Halloween Showdown

Somewhere in this mob, Peter Dramon was watching Jennifer, and waiting to make his move.

The music grew louder, the dancing more frenzied. Grotesque, beautiful, otherworldly faces swirled around her.

And suddenly, as if a switch had been thrown, it grew silent.

She saw him.

Eyes glittered, lips moved, the band worked drums, trumpets, and guitars without sounding a note.

He was there, in the middle of the floor.

Watching her.

Fairies and giants and dwarfs and mythical beasts spinning by in slow motion.

The floor seemed to ripple, Jennifer's legs buckled slightly at the knees.

She had wanted to throw a gauntlet in his face.

But he had tricked her.

Moving slowly toward her, gently pushing others aside. He wore no costume.

He was a wolf.

Green eyes glowing . . .

iBooks in the PRIVATE SCHOOL™ Series

Most iBooks are available at special quantity discounts for bulk purchases for sales promotions, premiums or fundraising. Special books or book excerpts can also be created to fit specific needs.
For details, email the publisher
@bricktower@aol.com

PRIVATE SCHOOL #6

THE LAST ALIEN

Steven Charles

A BYRON PREISS VISUAL PUBLICATIONS, INC.
BOOK

iBooks
Habent Sua Fata Libelli

iBooks
Manhanset House
Dering Harbor, New York 11965

bricktower@aol.com • www.ibooksinc.com

Library of Congress Cataloging-in-Publication Data
Charles, Steven. The last alien.
        (Private School) "A Byron Preiss book."
p. cm.
        [1. Young Adult Fiction—Horror. 2. Young Adult Fiction—Science
Fiction—Alien Contact. 3. Young Adult Fiction—Werewolfs and
Shifters.] I. Barr, Kenneth, ill. II. Title. III.
        Series: Charles, Steven. Private School.

ISBN 978-1-59687-735-1
December 2018

SPECIAL THANKS TO RON BUEHL,
PAT MACDONALD, MARJORIE
HANLON, AND DAVID M. HARRIS.
EDITOR—RUTH ASHBY

Table of Contents

One

THE EGYPTIAN QUEEN STOOD IN THE CENTER OF THE long, green-tiled corridor, her straight black hair banded in gold, her eyes outlined in green and vivid blue; copper bands encircled her upper arms, and a shimmering silver dress covered her to her bare feet.

She was angry.

And no one seemed to care.

With her hands on her hips, she looked behind her and then straight ahead, and folding her arms across her chest, she demanded to know—at the top of a shrill voice—which creep had swiped her good hairbrush. Immediately she was shoved to one side by a blond cowgirl and then again by a girl in red flannel pajamas. When she shouted a second time and no one answered, she threw up her hands in disgust and, with a curse, vanished back into her room.

Jennifer, who was standing in front of the door of her corner room, shook her head. "Royalty," she said, pretending to be sad, "gets no respect these days."

Beside her, sitting on the floor in the hall with her legs stretched out and her ankles crossed, Marysue Beauford only sneered. "Serves her right," she muttered. "She has worn that same stupid costume for the past two years, and I swear she really believes she's Cleopatra."

1

Jennifer leaned against the wall and slowly slid down to join her friend. "C'mon, she's not that bad."

Marysue nodded emphatically. "My dear," she said, her Virginia accent deliberately thickened, "if I were you, I had best practice my bowing and my scraping. That girl is one hard case when she's ignored."

Jennifer smiled, placed her forearms on her knees, and rested her chin thoughtfully on her arms. Almost immediately her smile began to fade, and the voices in the dormitory began to blend into a single droning noise. No words. No laughter. Just a noise that resembled the collective voice of a beehive.

And the girls readying themselves for bed or testing the effects of their Halloween costumes on anyone who would take the time to look, began to resemble grotesquely animated mannequins. Their flesh looked like plastic, their eyes like glass, and their smiles appeared to be painted on.

Echoes of distant thunder.

It's all right, she told herself then. Take it easy, it's all right.

A hand touched her arm gently, and when she couldn't return Marysue's smile, she pushed herself to her feet.

"I'm going downstairs," she said.

"Jen?"

"I just need some air, that's all. I'll be back in a few minutes."

And before Marysue could stop her, she hurried off to the front of the building and the staircase that led down to the entry hall, the double doors, and the open porch that ran along the front of the dorm.

A long, deep breath she released in a sigh.

It was just chilly enough to remind her that it was late October, but not so unpleasant that she was driven back inside. Instead she leaned against one of the porch posts and stared out over the campus lawn. Looking at, but not seeing the white globes of light that marked the edge of the circular drive, the occasional passing of a student. Just hearing the rumble of a lone truck on the highway beyond the gates of Thaler Academy. Catching the sharp scent of autumn on the still air.

Another sigh.

Then she looked to her left, to the far side of the crescent the main buildings formed. Beyond the last one were three houses. The first, partially obscured by the last dorm, was a large gingerbread Victorian that was the home of the dean, Peter Dramon. From where she stood she could see no lights, and she hadn't seen a light burning there since . . .

Where is he? she wondered.

Wishing now she had brought a jacket or a sweater, but not wanting to go back inside, she walked on the covered walkway that led to the Student Union, her heels loud on the planks, sharp and without echo. She moved briskly to warm herself, and when she reached the entrance, she looked through the front doors and changed her mind. There was nothing she wanted to do in there, either in the game room or the lounge.

And she definitely didn't feel like listening to yet another story about the natural gas explosion a week before. Half the student body thought the Russians had landed, others were positive there had been an earthquake.

The truth about the explosion, which only she and a few of her friends knew, had nothing to do with natural gas at all.

I wonder, she thought to herself as she headed back toward her dorm, if it's possible that it really is over.

This was something Marysue had been telling her for days.

The aliens were dead.

All of them.

The wolflike creatures had come there from a distant star to transform the earth's atmosphere into one resembling their own, a project that would have killed off all life on the planet save theirs. Scientists were calling the results of the aliens' project acid rain and industrial pollution. These they blamed for the dying forests of the world. Jennifer and her friends had discovered the real reason, and then they destroyed the aliens' underground laboratory and, they hoped, all of the aliens with it.

Pausing at the front door to the dorm, she glanced around again, wishing she could get rid of her restless feeling. It was driving her crazy, not being able to relax. She considered going down to the heated pool in the gymnasium to try to work off her tension with a few laps, but she changed her mind immediately when she thought of how cold she'd be when she left the heated water. Maybe a jog around the drive. Maybe a workout in the gymnastics room.

A scowl as she shook her head vigorously. This is silly, she thought. The next thing you know, kid, you'll want to climb a mountain.

A dark shadow passed over the face of the moon.

A sudden breeze hissed through the nearly leafless trees.

A dead leaf scuttled across the porch, its brittle edges scratching against the wood.

Suddenly she heard a noise around the corner of the two-story brick building. A footstep. Someone walking slowly toward the front.

For a moment panic blossomed in her chest and acid began to churn in her stomach.

They're not all dead, she thought. Oh, no, they're not all dead!

Then, as she reached for the door to throw herself inside, a tall girl with books cradled in her arms popped around the corner, gasped when she saw Jennifer, and laughed with embarrassment as she walked on toward the Student Union.

Jennifer stared after her, somewhat breathlessly, and felt silly.

Nice going, Field, she told herself as she hurried inside. You're going to start turning shadows into monsters soon if you're not careful. Nevertheless, she couldn't stop herself from shivering, remembering how the aliens had been able to pass themselves off as humans, how three of her classmates had actually been *them*.

Gone now. Forever. Their disappearances had added to the excitement of the past week—rumor had Barbara O'Malley dropping out of school, which surprised very few since the redhead had not been known for her scholastic achievement. And Monica Holt? Some had her in New York because of a modeling offer, and others had her running off with the dean. Hardly anyone cared about the disappearance of Esther Fine—but someone said she had gone home to take care of her sick mother.

Through all of it, Jennifer and Marysue had feigned interest and said nothing. Told none of them the truth.

In fact, they themselves had been the focus of gossip as well. The Staines police had falsely accused them of being part of a ring of burglars. But the word was out now that they had been working secretly with the authorities to catch the burglars. They became, for the past week, somewhat famous, and that attention Jennifer could have done without.

She grinned at the thought as she climbed the stairs. She grinned more widely when she saw Marysue still sitting on the floor, arguing heatedly with Cleopatra about the amount of cleavage that would be permitted at the Halloween dance.

"Honey," Beauford called to the girl's back. "You want to give all those poor boys heart failure? Have a little compassion."

Jennifer stood over her. "You the fashion expert around here now?"

"I do what I can for the less fortunate among us," was the answer. "Speaking of which, are you all right?"

Jennifer knelt and shrugged. "I guess so."

Marysue put a hand on her arm. "You gotta relax, girl, you gotta relax."

"But I keep thinking about . . ." She looked over her shoulder, remembering the girl on the porch. "You know. I can't seem to get it out of my head."

Marysue nodded slowly. "I know. Believe me, I know. But it's done now, Jenny," she said earnestly. "I mean, no one will ever know what we did. And if they do find out, they won't believe it. I don't even believe it half the time myself. But it's done. We did it. Now we have to forget. There is life after saving the world, you know."

Jennifer knew the girl was right. Yet she also knew there was still one, major unanswered question—where was Peter Dramon? They had never learned whether the dean of Thaler Academy had actually been one of the aliens or was only working for them. And they still didn't know if he had been killed in the explosion with the others, or if he was still free.

Marysue stared at her, a half smile on her lips. "I know you want to talk to him, but thinking about him isn't going to make him appear in your room," she said quietly.

Jennifer started, wondering how Beauford had been able to read her mind.

"So what do we do about it?" she asked.

"Not a thing, child," Marysue said decisively. "Not a blessed, wonderful thing."

"But—"

Marysue took a quick deep breath and pushed herself to her feet. "Look," she said as Jennifer rose as well, "if he's one of them, one of those *things,* he'll die soon enough without the proper equipment to give him the atmosphere he needs, right? And if he's one of us, he's going to have to work for a living now, right?" She nodded sharply. "Right. So what's the problem?"

"None, I guess."

"You guessed right!" Marysue applauded. "You win the grand prize."

"Which is?"

"Figuring out what I'm going to wear to the stupid dance on Friday." She pointed down the hall toward Cleopatra, who was posing against the wall for another girl holding a camera. "I mean, if Zucco comes and sees something like that, he's not going to look at me all night."

Jennifer laughed heartily and liked it. It was a good feeling, a grand one, a sense of relief she'd been trying for since the whole nightmarish episode had ended, out there in the forest.

"I'll think about it," she said.

"Well, think hard, Field, think hard. I only have three days, you know."

Three days, she thought as she returned to the peace of her room a few minutes later. Three days.

She didn't have the faintest idea what to go as. She had considered and rejected everything from a simple ghost to a character from history. She just didn't know.

Finally she stood in front of her mirror and examined herself from all angles, trying to ignore the signs of weariness that no amount of makeup could cover, trying to forget all the sleepless nights she had suffered.

She piled her auburn hair on top of her head and lowered her eyelids in an attempt to look seductive; she put her hands on her hips and tried to look tough; she made faces, crossed her eyes, and began to giggle.

"Crazy," she said to her reflection. "You are crazy!"

She didn't turn when someone knocked on her door, she only made another face in the mirror and shouted, "The door's open."

So that she didn't see whoever it was who came in and softly hissed behind her, "Now I've got you, Field. Now you're going to die!"

She didn't see it until she whirled around and found herself looking directly into the face of a wolf.

Green eyes glowing.

Two

WITH HER WORST NIGHTMARE COME TRUE, JENNIFER was unable to act. She stood frozen in terror, her mind a blank, her limbs turned to stone.

The wolf stood on its hind legs in the middle of the small room, snarling and hissing, swaying from side to side. "You're going to die!" it said again.

Jennifer swallowed and pressed back against the dresser, blinking rapidly, unable to break eye contact with the creature.

Then it took a step toward her.

Jennifer shook her head, breaking the spell the wolf had cast.

It tossed its head, stepped to one side, and crouched as if it were going to spring at her throat.

Just at that moment Marysue charged through the door, grabbed the creature around the waist, and threw it onto the bed. She fell on top of it and tried to get her hands around its throat.

Only then did Jennifer shake off her fear. She grabbed a hairbursh from the dresser, ran to the wrestling, grunting figures, and raised the brush over them like a club.

And stopped.

Marysue was pummeling the thing, but the wolf was laughing and shrieking for her to stop before she ruined everything.

"Oh, no," Jennifer said in disgust and relief, noting for the first time that the wolf was wearing a pair of dark jeans. "Beauford," she said sharply. "Beauford, stop it!"

Marysue, tangled in the sheets and blanket, looked up and blinked. Then she sat up, shoved the creature away, and glared as it reached up to take off its head.

"No," Jennifer said again and sagged against the dresser.

"You know," said Marty Visran, "I thought it was a good costume, but not this good. You nearly killed me, Beauford."

Marty was a tall, slender sophomore from California, with an abundance of freckles and hair so blond it was nearly white. Right then her face was flushed from her exertion. She asked, "What gives, anyway? You guys on something or what?"

Jennifer picked up the wolf head and examined it. The green eyes were painted on, the actual eyeholes were where the wolf's nostrils would be. She couldn't help it, she began to giggle.

Marysue only trembled.

Jennifer began to hiccough, too.

Marty hooted with laughter as she shook out her hair. "You are on something! You are! You guys—" She stood and looked around the room. "What is it? You got beer, scotch, drugs, what? C'mon, what?"

"Nothing, Marty, really," Jennifer insisted, but the more she tried to calm herself, the more she giggled. Her eyes began to water. Her chest began to ache. It was hysteria, and she knew it, yet she was unable to control it;

and Marty's frantic hunt around the room for the liquor she was sure was hidden there only made it worse.

Finally Marysue grabbed Marty's arm, pulled her away just as she was about to open the closet, and led her firmly to the door. "You heard the lady, Marty. We got nothing here for the peasants."

"Oh, sure," she said, winking at Jennifer. "Well, at least I know my costume works. Neat, huh? Thanks!"

When she was gone, Marysue slammed the door and dropped onto the bed.

"Creep," she said.

Jennifer hiccoughed again, clamped a hand over her mouth, and staggered to her desk chair, turning it away from the casement window to face her bed. "It's not her fault," she managed to get out. "She doesn't know."

"Well—" Marysue sniffed, then pushed her hands back through her black hair. "I guess."

"Hey, you were the one who told me to relax, remember?"

"Yeah, well, how was I to know she wasn't—" And she slapped the mattress, hard.

Jennifer closed her eyes briefly, recalling her own inability to act when Marty came into the room. She wondered what had happened, why she had been unable to move. Even at the most frightening and dangerous times during the past couple of months, she had never behaved like that. Usually it was Marysue who froze while she acted.

That time their roles had been reversed.

Marysue stretched out on the bed and pillowed her hands behind her head. "I think," she said to the ceiling, "I'm going to cut classes to be with Zucco tomorrow."

Jennifer looked at her, the color only then beginning to return to Marysue's face. "You sure you want to cut?"

"Yeah."

Zucco was the nickname for Marysue's boyfriend, Conrad Chang, who along with Lee Fawkes formed the rest of the quartet that had done most of the work in defeating the aliens. Although Jennifer would not call Lee her boyfriend, something more than the shared experience of their adventure held them together. It might have been because they had a common background. Most of the girls at Thaler were wealthy, such as the Visran twins, whose California family owned half the West Coast. But she and Lee had to earn their way through school with scholarships and part-time jobs. Their bond might also have something specifically to do with Lee. One minute he was tough and unconcerned, but at the next he demonstrated, however briefly, a sensitivity and vulnerability that made him quite special to her.

She hadn't had the time to explore any of her reactions to Lee and their relationship before because of their troubles, but now she knew she was going to have to. It didn't look as if Lee would be going away, and she definitely knew she didn't want him to.

"Tell you what," Marysue said, color returning at last to her cheeks, "why don't we both go into town tomorrow."

"When?"

"For supper. At the Hilltop. We'll call the guys, trick them into paying, and then watch them squirm when we ask them to take us to the movies." She grinned. Then laughed.

"That's not nice," Jennifer said, only half scolding.

"I know, but it's fun."

"Marysue!"

Beauford shrugged, rolled to her feet, and made a pro-
duction out of yawning. "Well, my dear, you think about
it. Meanwhile, it's time for us Richmond elite to get our
beauty sleep, not that we need it, you understand. And
while you dream, try to come up with something I can
wear to the dance, okay?"

"What about me?" Jennifer said as her friend stepped
into the hall.

Marysue looked over her shoulder. "You?"

Jennifer nodded.

"Well, frankly, Scarlett, I don't give a . . ."

Jennifer scooped up a book and threw it at her; she
laughed when the door slammed and the book landed
harmlessly on the floor. Taking a deep breath, she turned
the chair around to stare out the window at the hills
behind the campus. At the stars she could see beyond the
reflection of her room in the panes.

Then she thought about Marty Visran and hoped
Marty's twin sister, Amy, wasn't going as a wolf as well.
It would be bad enough seeing one of them.

She yawned.

She decided she might as well go to bed.

An hour later she gave up staring at the ceiling and
waiting for sleep to sneak up on her.

It had been that way for a week. She would lie there,
forcing herself not to think, and failing; demanding that
her imagination take a vacation, and failing; telling herself that all was well at last, and knowing that she
couldn't prove it.

She had to know.

She had to know about Dramon.

After putting on her jeans and shoes, she pulled on a
heavy sweater and grabbed her jacket from the closet.

Then she turned out the lights and took several slow breaths to calm herself. There was no need to bring a weapon; she was only going to look, not to explore.

A check of the hallway—it was dim, quiet, only the sound of a dripping faucet down in the shower room, only the sound of her own breathing.

She waited, just to be sure.

And as she did, she told herself she was being foolish. If Dramon hadn't been killed in the explosion or hadn't suffocated in what was to him alien air, then all that his absence meant was that he was scrambling about, trying to get his human life back in order. Any day then he would make himself known with some story about having been on a trip. And when he did return, there would be nothing she could do. Nothing any of them could do.

Over, she told herself. One way or another, it's over.

But she couldn't wait.

She had to know, if only to help send her nightmares away.

For a brief moment she considered getting Marysue to go with her, then changed her mind because she already knew her answer and didn't need the lecture she knew would accompany it.

When she was positive the dorm was settled for the night, she moved silently to the fire exit door, pushed through it, and ran down the steps to the ground floor. A pause as she listened for the sound of anyone following, and then she was out the side door and running to the back of the building.

The cold had worsened; already there were signs of frost on the grass.

Quickly, with head down and hands deep in her jacket pockets, she made her way along the rear of the buildings in the crescent, staying in the dark and out of the ghostly squares of light thrown by windows above her.

The hills that rose behind the campus blended with the nightsky, and the forest that covered them whispered to her in the wind.

When she reached the last building, a dormitory, she checked to be sure no one was watching and moved closer to stare across the lawn at the three houses. The two farthest from her, lighted and warm looking, were used by those faculty members who didn't have rooms in Staines, the town down in the valley; the nearest one was the dean's.

Every night for a week she had stood in that spot, in the shadows, watching the house.

Wondering if anything was going on behind the dark windows.

The night before had been the worst. The urge to walk over to it and simply knock on the door had been almost too great to resist. Only the fear of coming face to face with him had held her back.

A distant keening as the wind rose over the hills.

She let her mind drift, and she thought of Pauline Klopher at her desk in the library. But the older woman, part of the group that had uncovered and destroyed the alien plot, had said good-bye to Jennifer a few days earlier. Time away, the woman had explained, looking even older than usual; she needed time away, and time to recover.

She wouldn't be back until after the first of the next month.

The rustle of wings overhead, something dark in the nightsky heading for the woods.

Bordon Overbrook, the ecology instructor who had been the second adult to believe her story, couldn't help her now either; he was dead—she was sure of it—killed in a fight with one of the creatures.

She tried not to keep track of time; it passed too slowly already. Nor did she allow herself to go over all the events that had led to her vigil; they had become the nightmares that woke her drenched in perspiration.

She simply waited.

Listening to the October night whisper and mutter to itself.

Until suddenly she blinked and leaned closer, her throat dry and her hands out of her pockets, in fists at her sides.

There was a light.

On the second floor there was a light in Dramon's house that had snapped off the moment after she rubbed her eyes to look again.

Three

JENNIFER WOKE UP WEDNESDAY MORNING, NOT IN stages as she usually did, but suddenly, with all sleep vanished in an instant. She sat straight up in bed and stared at the bright light pouring in through her windows. Her head was clear, and after she had rubbed her eyes and yawned once, she noticed her coat and sweater on her desk chair.

And she remembered the light.

It wasn't a dream, she thought, pushing both hands back through her hair.

"I saw it," she whispered. And she smiled broadly. "I really saw it."

There was no terror.

There was only the memory of the burning lamp in the dean's shaded window.

And by the time she had dressed and was seated in her first class of the morning, her mind was racing, and she paid little attention to the earnest young instructor trying to explain the subtleties of Shakespeare. And then the first rush of excitement faded.

It was odd.

All that time she had been preparing for fear, for a wave of horror, for anything but this nearly giddy and overwhelming sense of relief. She supposed it had been all the waiting and the uncertainty. Anticipating the dean's return had produced more anxieties than she could handle. It had been not knowing—was he or wasn't he dead?

And now that she was positive of the answer, the anxieties were vanishing. And now she was ready to take the next step.

Marysue didn't believe it when she heard the story over lunch in the Student Union dining hall.

"It's obvious, child. You were sleepwalking," she said, grimacing at a soggy sandwich that was supposed to be grilled cheese.

"I wasn't. I was wide-awake."

"It was on the second floor?"

She nodded quickly.

Marysue shook her head. "Sorry. You were just sleeping. You went out there and you fell asleep on your feet."

"I was *not* asleep!"

Marysue quickly scanned the crowded room and shook her head slowly. "Then you were imagining it, Jen. You wanted to see a light, so you did." She grinned and lifted her hands, palms up. "As simple as that."

"I saw a light," she insisted.

Marysue said nothing.

And before Jennifer could explain further, Amy Visran came up with her sister and asked if it were true that Marty had scared the pants off Jennifer with a stupid wolf costume.

"Right," Marysue said before Jennifer could answer. "It was stupid."

"Hey, I don't think so, Beauford," Marty said with a grin. "As a matter of fact, Amy's decided she doesn't want to be Little Red Riding Hood now. She's gonna be a wolf too. Isn't that great?"

"Super," said Beauford sourly. "Now go eat a lamb or something, we're trying to talk here."

Jennifer watched the twins wend their way toward the door, giggling, chattering, and looking over their shoulders every few steps. Then she turned her full attention back to Marysue, who immediately raised a hand.

"Don't," the girl said. "You're killing what's left of my appetite."

And she didn't believe it when Jennifer insisted it wasn't her imagination while they were seated one behind the other in their art appreciation class.

"How could he just come back like that?" Beauford whispered over her shoulder.

"I don't know."

The instructor arranged reproductions of famous portraits on easels at the front of the room. He took up a pointer, cleared his throat, and resumed his nasal droning.

"I mean, it's not like he's got an army behind him anymore," Marysue said from the corner of her mouth.

"I know."

"Maybe it's not him."

"Who else would it be?"

"How should I know? The cleaning lady maybe."

"In the middle of the night?"

"There's always a first time."

"Marysue Beauford, you are impossible!"

"Not me, child. I'm not the one who's seeing phantom lights in an empty house."

"But—"

"Ladies," the instructor said with a cold smile, "would you mind conducting your personal business on your own time? We do have a class in session, in case you've forgotten."

Jennifer slumped back in her seat and glared at Marysue's back, wishing she could go back in time to drag the stubborn girl out of her bed to show her. Just show her.

She leaned forward. "It *was* him!"

"Miss Field!" the instructor snapped.

Marysue's shoulders shook as she stifled a laugh.

They sat in the common room of their dormitory on a deep, comfortable couch that faced the front windows. Behind them a handful of girls were eagerly watching a bad late-afternoon film, and at one of the tables a group was playing bridge with more good-humored arguing than skill. On the wall near the entrance was a large poster announcing the Halloween dance, with the unnecessary reminder that gentlemen were permitted.

"I don't know," Marysue said, her hands twisting in her lap.

"What do you mean, you don't know? You have to know!"

"I do not."

Jennifer grabbed one of her hands and held it still. "Listen, Marysue, I saw what I saw, and you *know* it wasn't my imagination."

She waited.

Finally, with great reluctance, Marysue nodded.

"So?"

Marysue sighed.

Jennifer smiled. "It's the only way, and you know it."

A shriek of laughter from the girls around the television, a chorus of "Be quiet!" from the card players.

"But why do we have to sneak around in the middie of the night?" Marysue asked. "Why don't we just walk up there and knock on his door?"

"Because," she said patiently, "if we just knock on the door and he answers, he won't ask us in. And we have to know what's going on in there. We have to know if he's up to something. And the only way we can do that is by getting inside."

"We," Marysue said flatly.

Jennifer looked away. "All right. Me. But I can't do it myself."

"We," Marysue repeated and managed a weak smile when Jennifer looked back at her. "You think I'm going to be able to sleep any better knowing he's back? What are you crazy, Field? You think you're in this all by your lonesome?"

Jennifer wanted to hug her.

"I hate this," Marysue said as they stood and headed for the telephones on the hall wall. "I really hate this."

"By tomorrow morning it'll be all over, one way or the other."

"I don't like the sound of that."

"Call," Jennifer said, handing her a receiver. "Tell Zucco we'll meet him and Lee at the Hilltop around six-thirty tonight. And tell him it's our treat."

Beauford winced. "This will be bad for my image, Field, you realize that?"

"Trust me," Jennifer said, heading for the stairs.

"I did that once before," Marysue called after her. "And look at all the trouble you got me into."

Jennifer laughed and ran all the way to her room. It was crazy, but a feeling of excitement had returned. She wasn't making light of the possible dangers because she had already been close to death many times and knew the fear. She was also aware that her friends were facing the same dangers as well. But she was certain, now that

Marysue had confessed, that none of them was going to be able to rest until every alien and alien collaborator had been accounted for.

Conrad had said that without a life-support system, the creatures would die.

Perhaps.

But there was always the remote possibility that there was something they didn't know, something they had missed; and if they missed it, it could mean their lives.

She washed, changed her clothes, and vigorously brushed her long auburn hair. Lee had been aloof since the night they blew up the alien den. He was coming to the couple of classes he was taking at Thaler, but he had had little to say to her. He was friendly enough, but he acted distracted, and she needed to find out that night if, somehow, his affection for her had changed.

No, she told herself sharply. Don't start thinking like that. He's only trying to work things out, that's all. He was as affected as I was. It's nothing more than that.

After she grabbed her coat and a pair of gloves, she banged on Marysue's door and told her she'd wait in the parking lot, ran downstairs and hurried out to the porch. The walkways between the buildings were crowded—students were leaving late classes, heading for dinner in the Union, or going to the library or the gymnasium. A large van was backed up against the curb, and a workman was carrying cartons of books into the Union, bound for the bookstore. A few cars were driving slowly around the drive, stopping to pick up passengers for an evening in Staines.

She glanced at her watch. Five minutes to go. And when her stomach grumbled, she decided to grab a roll from the dining hall, something to nibble on until she got into town.

The white globes around the drive snapped on as she walked, deepening the twilight, making the dormant grass in the center appear more brittle.

The back doors of the van were slammed shut from the inside, and as she walked past the van the red glow from the taillights appeared harsh when the brakes were applied.

A breeze gusted under the roof, pushing her hair into her eyes.

After walking into the dining room, she changed her mind about the roll, stepped outside again and down to the narrow band of grass rimming the drive, and followed the blacktop's curve toward the parking lot on the far side. She kept her head down, fumbling into her gloves as she stepped off the curb and onto the drive. She looked up only when a car honked as it passed her.

A glance over her shoulder to see if Marysue was coming.

A look ahead at the student parking lot. The lamp-posts surrounding it were on then, and they turned the windshields frosty white and caused the red and amber reflectors to glow. At the moment no one was there, but she could see, even from there, the bright red of Beauford's old, bullet-shaped Thunderbird, and she quickened her step.

An engine coughed to life behind her.

She wondered what Lee would think about her wanting to break into the dean's house, then decided that she didn't want to know, not just then. She could never guess how he'd respond.

The engine raced.

Field, she thought, give it up. You're never going to be able to figure him out.

Which, she supposed, was a great deal of his attraction.

Then she grinned when she saw Marysue appear from behind her red car in the lot. And faltered when the girl suddenly began waving her arms frantically. Even though she was calling, Jennifer couldn't hear her because the engine noise behind her was too loud.

She turned around and froze.

It was the van.

Its headlights were out, and it was moving around the curve, straight for her.

She backed up, not believing it.

Can't the fool see me? she thought and waved her arms above her head.

The van kept coming.

The rear tires shrieked as the vehicle suddenly picked up speed, headlights flaring on and blinding her as it swung around the curve.

Jennifer whirled to run, had taken only a step before she tripped in her panic. Her hands scraped along the blacktop, her knees exploded with pain, and when she looked back, the van was only a few yards behind her.

Four

THE ROAR OF THE ENGINE WAS THE ONLY SOUND SHE heard, its glaring lights all she saw.

Two thoughts rose simultaneously in her brain: the idiot! and, I'm going to die.

Then panic blossomed again, and she rolled swiftly to one side as the vehicle bellowed past, and she came quickly up on her knees to watch it race down the drive and out the gateless pillars that marked the academy's entrance.

In an instant it was gone, the taillights vanishing as if a great beast had closed its eyes.

Jennifer kept on staring, watching the taillights, hearing the engine, saying nothing when Marysue ran up to her and dropped to her side.

"You okay?"

She nodded mutely.

"That jackass could've killed you!"

Marysue rose and slipped her hands under Jennifer's arms and gently pulled her to her feet.

Jennifer didn't protest when Marysue dusted off her jacket; she waited until her lungs and heart started working normally again before looking at her hands. She winced. There were bits of stone and dirt clinging to her palms, and the stinging finally made itself known.

Gingerly she brushed her fingers over the skin, blowing on the palms, and finally sighing when she saw there was no blood.

"Idiot," Marysue muttered as they walked to the car. "He was steering right for you. Couldn't he see you?"

Marysue unlocked the car, and Jennifer climbed in and felt a sudden weakness overtake her, a reaction to the near accident. She rolled the window down and let the cool air slap her face as Marysue pulled out of the lot and down the drive.

"He was carrying books," Jennifer said once they were on the highway that led down into the valley.

"What?"

"Books. He was carrying books. I saw him bringing a carton into the Union."

Marysue looked at her, then back to the road.

The road was dark now, with no streetlights or houses; the moon still on the rise. Jennifer listened to the whirr of the tires over the asphalt and took in the night air in great gulps. By the time they had reached the valley floor, she was sitting up again and, though still a bit shaken, feeling much better.

"Eskimo," Marysue said.

Jennifer looked at her. "What?"

"You're part Eskimo, right?" And she pointed at the window.

Jennifer just grinned.

"Well, child, I am from the South, remember? Richmond only allows cold in the winter months. Its citizens are too delicate."

"This is Connecticut," Jennifer said, rolling the window up, leaving an inch at the top. "Its citizens are not quite so fragile."

"More's the pity."

The houses began then, and a few blocks later the business district. Luckily, Marysue found a parking space only a few doors shy of the Hilltop Luncheonette, and by the time she had locked the doors and joined Jennifer on the sidewalk, two boys were walking toward them.

Lee Fawkes was dressed in black denim and a dark leather jacket, his sandy hair tossed by the wind. As he walked there was a faint hint of a swagger, a silent challenge to anyone who might get in his way. Jennifer grinned at him and waved, and suddenly he looked shy, as if he didn't know how to respond to the young woman who faced him.

He was tall, but was dwarfed by Conrad Chang, whose bulk and height were exaggerated by his sheepskin jacket and gray western hat that covered his blond hair. His light coloring and height he took from his mother, and his vaguely Oriental features came from his father's side. He had an exotic look that Marysue—and others—found irresistible.

She took his arm as soon as he stepped up to her and said, "We are starving, Zucco, so let's go. Besides, there's an idiot in a van who seems to be hunting Jennifer out of season."

Lee's face instantly darkened, and Jennifer, holding his hand tightly, explained what had happened as they went into the luncheonette and found themselves a booth near the center of the right-hand wall. When she finished, he was glowering, and she knew that given half a chance he would spend the rest of the night combing Staines for the driver, hoping to rearrange his face.

"I'm all right," she insisted when he asked her for the tenth time. "Really. He just shook me up a bit, that's all."

Across the table Marysue shrugged out of her jacket
and crammed it against the wall. "Maybe he should have
nicked you a little."

Jennifer gaped at her.

"Oh, not bad. Just enough to put you to bed, where
you belong."

"What kind of a crack is that?" Lee demanded.

"Hey, don't get all bent out of shape," she said. "I just
said—."

"I know what you said," he snapped.

"Yeah, but I'll give you five bucks if you don't agree
when you hear what she's up to this time."

Conrad, bemused, signaled the waitress.

Jennifer couldn't help giggling, which only made Lee
more angry. "What's going on?" he demanded quietly.

A deep breath and a look at Beauford. "There was a
light in Dramon's house last night," she said.

Lee looked at her for a long time before whispering,
"Damn."

Her story had to wait, however, because the waitress
came just then to take their order. Conrad, after making
sure that Marysue's offer of picking up the check still
held, suggested that the woman just begin at the top of
the menu and continue to bring food until he cried uncle.
Beauford punched his arm. He laughed, stopped when he
realized the waitress didn't think he was funny, and
ordered the Hilltop hamburger special, which Jennifer
knew was enough to feed any two or three normal
people.

When the waitress left, Marysue nodded. "The special," she said glumly. "I should have known."

"I'm hungry," he protested.

"You're always hungry," she grumbled.

"I am a growing boy, Richmond, and don't you forget it."

"You're a whale in a blond wig, that's what you are."

Jennifer laughed and suggested that that was what he ought to go as, to the dance. Then she turned to Lee. "What about you? You made up your mind yet?"

He shrugged and glanced down the line of customers at the counter. "I don't know. I think it's silly."

"Lee!"

"Well, it is, you know? That's kid stuff, dressing up like ghosts and things."

Marysue rolled her eyes.

Conrad leaned over and said, "My mother's making me this great cape, Fawkes, wait till you see it. Best-dressed vampire you ever saw. After the dance I'm going to get a part-time job in a blood bank."

Lee looked at him in disgust. "Wonderful."

"Vat is this?" Conrad asked in his best Count Dracula voice. "You do not believe in the undead?"

Lee attempted a slight smile.

Jennifer touched Lee's arm until he looked at her. "What's the matter?" she asked quietly.

"Nothing." He stared at his hands folded on the table.

"Right. You're being a jerk for nothing, is that it? I thought you wanted to go. In fact, as I recall, you asked me to go with you."

He couldn't maintain his gloomy look; a brief smile parted his lips. "You asked me."

"I did?" she said in exaggerated surprise. "Was I that bold, that forward, that—"

"Jesse James," he said then.

"I was Jesse James?"

"No, I'm Jesse James."

"No, you're not . . . Oh," she said, one hand to her cheek. "I get it! You're going as Jesse James!"

He raised a fist and touched it lightly to the point of her chin.

"An outlaw," Marysue said with a nod. "That figures."

"What's that supposed to mean?" he asked.

And Jennifer sighed, loud enough for both of them to stop and look at her for a moment. Lee and Marysue, in spite of all they had been through together, still managed to get on each other's nerves now and then, mostly because of Lee and his inability to deal with his envy of her family's wealth and position. They did like each other, but Lee couldn't always understand why.

"Were you saying something, Miss Field?" Conrad asked, still using his Dracula voice.

"Yes, about the light in Dramon's window. I have a plan."

"Nuts," Marysue grumbled. "I thought you'd forgotten it. Foiled again."

Lee half turned, pulling up a leg to rest on the seat.

"There really was a light?" he asked, keeping his voice low.

She nodded.

Conrad said, "He's back, then?"

"I don't know. Somebody is."

"I know exactly what she's going to say, since she practiced on me already. And I want to go on record, right now, as saying that her idea is silly and dangerous—but you're not going to listen to me anyway, so I don't know why I even bother."

"Right," the others said together and laughed.

But the laughter was short.

Before she even spoke, the boys knew what her idea was—to break into the dean's house and have a look around. She told them that it had nothing to do with saving the world or anything like that.

It was peace of mind.

It was the burial of nightmares.

"I just have to know how he fits into all this," she said after their meals had been delivered and sorted out. "And for all our sakes, not just mine, I want to make sure he's not planning anything else."

"But how will we know that?" Lee asked.

"I don't know exactly, but we should be able to tell if there has been any unusual activity there."

"But they're all dead," Conrad reminded her.

"And what could Dramon do?" Marysue asked. "If he's alone, he can't do a thing."

"I don't know that they're all dead," she answered. "And I have to. Don't you understand?"

Their silence told her that they understood completely. They didn't like it, but they understood.

They ate in silence, and she wondered if perhaps she really was being ridiculous, overly concerned. And now that she had brought her fear into the open, she began to have second thoughts. Serious ones she could not reconcile with the sudden and inexplicable feeling of dread that crept over her, making her shiver, making her shift back into the corner of the booth and hug herself.

Conrad stared at them. "It smells like smoke in here, you know that?"

Lee glanced over toward the counter. "Something must be burning on the grill."

Jennifer scarcely heard them. She was staring over their heads at the door to the kitchen at the far end of the counter, not seeing anything until, suddenly, something seemed wrong.

Very wrong.

A few other customers began to complain about the smell.

Marysue twisted around and knelt, looking over the back of the booth.

She dropped back down and shrugged.

"Lee," Jennifer said then, in a small voice.

Suddenly a man dressed in grease-stained white burst out of the kitchen, shouting. For a second no one paid any attention to him. Then they looked at him as he raced up the aisle, and Marysue gasped when she saw the row of flames along his back.

Before anyone could react or move to help him, he plunged through the door, and at the same time, something exploded in the kitchen, and a huge ball of fire billowed into the shop.

Five

THE FORCE OF THE EXPLOSION WASN'T SO GREAT AS the noise it made, but it was enough to slam Jennifer against the wall and almost throw Conrad out of his seat.

Immediately the rear wall was covered in flame, and a moment later the luncheonette was filled with thick, roiling smoke. Lee grabbed Jennifer's arm and yanked her out of the booth, shouting to her to hurry as the fire began to make its way along the counter. She choked on the smoke, gagged on the smell, and was nearly torn from his grasp when another customer collided with her and both fell to the floor. They quickly regained their feet.

A fire alarm rang.

Glasses shattered like gunshots from the sudden high heat.

A young man was lying unconscious by the door, and Lee released Jennifer's hand to reach down and grab him by the jacket and drag him out into the street. With her eyes stinging and her chest heaving as if it would explode, she stumbled to the curb, where someone else immediately put an arm around her waist and led her quickly down the street and away from the restaurant. She tried to find Lee and the others, but she could see nothing except smoke pouring out of the door and racing for the sky; then the plate glass window shattered, and more smoke billowed out—black and gray, sweeping out over the street.

She felt like screaming.

Finally the man who had grabbed her asked if she were all right; he asked her again, anxiously, when she didn't respond at once. Then she looked at him for the first time and saw that he was a policeman. After a moment she nodded. He told her to stay where she was, and he ran back toward the Hilltop, one arm thrown up over his face as he plunged back inside.

Bile charged into her throat then, and she turned and retched into the gutter, her left hand braced against the fender of a car. It felt as if her entire stomach were trying to rip itself apart, and tears flooded over her cheeks until, at last, it was over and she was gulping for air.

Voices shouting and crying created such a din that it made her want to run away, anywhere but there.

Someone called her name.

She blinked slowly and looked to her left; Lee and a hatless Conrad were running toward her, their clothes covered with the residue of smoke and ash. As soon as she flung herself into Lee's arms, Conrad realized that Jennifer was alone; Marysue wasn't with her. He turned to run back to the Hilltop. By then, however, there was a crowd gathering, and outnumbered police were trying to move it away from the danger. Fire engines wailed to the scene, cruisers with lights spinning parked at all angles on the blacktop, and a patrolman brusquely ordered them to the other side of the street once he knew that Jennifer was all right.

Conrad refused to go, shouting Marysue's name.

The man said sternly, but not unkindly, "There's nothing you can do for your friend now. Just get over there before you get hurt! I'm sure she's all right. But you're in the way. You have to move."

"But she was with me, and I had her hand, but something happened and . . ."

After exchanging worried glances, Jennifer and Lee each took him by an arm, and when he looked at them in turn, his eyes were filled with tears, his face smeared with sooty smoke.

"C'mon, Zucco," Lee said quietly, pulling him toward the opposite curb. "She's all right, don't worry. She'll turn up. We'll find her."

Jennifer felt like crying again, but there was too much chaos then as the assault on the fire struggled to organize itself, and there was nothing they could do but watch the fire fighters go about their business.

Another patrol car screamed up; the movie theater was being evacuated.

An ambulance arrived on the scene, and several white-coated attendants leaped out of the back.

"I had her," Conrad said dully.

Lee said nothing.

"I had her, and then we got separated. I don't know what happened."

Jennifer watched as the medics broke through the crowd of police and firemen on the other side, carrying someone on a stretcher. She tried to see who was lying there. Conrad did, too, and he sobbed once with relief when they both saw it was a man.

Streams of water were aimed into the Hilltop and at the roof of the two-story building and at those on the buildings alongside it. A stout man in uniform was issuing instructions with a bullhorn. Barricades were set up to keep the crowds from getting into the street.

The ambulance left, its siren wailing.

"I had her," Conrad repeated, his voice now a harsh whisper.

"It's okay," Lee said calmly, straining to see through the crowds. "She's probably looking tor you, too. Why don't we—."

But Conrad was already gone, elbowing his way through the spectators, calling Marysue's name.

Jennifer leaned against Lee and felt his arm go around her waist.

"She'll be okay," he said again. "What about you?"

"It all happened so fast," she said weakly. "I don't even know what happened."

"I'll bet it was a grease fire or something," he said almost absently. "Something caught fire on the grill and the guy tried to put it out himself. Remember last August, when there was a fire here also. It was a grease fire then."

"But the explosion."

He shrugged. "I don't know. Gas maybe. I just don't know."

She wanted to argue, to tell him she hadn't smelled any gas, but suddenly it didn't matter. Not now. She pushed his arm gently away and took his hand, looked at him, and he nodded—standing there they wouldn't find their friend.

They pushed their way through the chattering, excited crowd, searching every face, every few feet stopping and trying to see across the street to spot Marysue. The smoke had lessened considerably now, no flames could be seen, and Jennifer noticed that the frantic activities of the fire fighters had lessened as well. A couple of them, wearing gas masks, dragged a heavy hose into the shop; two others were busily clearing the rest of the glass from the front window.

A second ambulance.

She spotted a fireman lying in the street, a colleague leaning over him holding an oxygen mask over the man's nose and talking to him with a lopsided smile.

But there was no sign of Marysue.

At the end of the block they were able to step off the curb into the street, but a policeman, although sympathetic to their concern, refused to permit them to cross to the other side. When Lee pressed, the man promised to keep an eye out for Marysue and immediately hurried away.

"I haven't even seen Zucco," Jennifer said as they backed away from the worst of the crowd.

Then the crowd parted to let the second ambulance through, and Lee gripped her arm tightly. She followed his gaze and gasped—through the back window of the emergency vehicle, she saw Conrad, leaning over someone on a stretcher.

The hospital for Staines and the surrounding area was only six blocks away, and Jennifer and Lee ran the entire distance. For a while Jennifer felt as if she were swimming upstream, moving against the flow of the curious who were still heading to the fire. Twice she collided with someone else, and once she was shoved by a man who shouted at her before she hurried on.

And as she ran, keeping her eye on Lee's back, she couldn't help but see the fire at the Hilltop superimposed over an image of the aliens' laboratory bursting into flame underground. She slowed almost to a walk as the thought struck her that the two might be related.

Then she shook her head to dismiss the idea and ran on, following Lee around a corner and down a quiet

street. An ambulance was heading in the opposite direction, and when she glanced at it, she saw that it was
empty.

The hospital, midway down the block, was a three-
story building of brick and simulated marble, the emergency entrance on the near side, under a portico. Lee was
already inside when she ran panting up the slanted drive
and through the electronic double doors. He was standing
in the middle of a large room, his shoulders rising and
falling as he took in great gulps of air.

Directly ahead was a long counter behind which a
handful of nurses and an intern were working at com-
puter terminals and talking to an attendant whom Jennifer had seen at the fire. Left and right were sections
marked off as waiting areas, and from them corridors led
deeper into the building itself.

Conrad was nowhere in sight.

Neither was Marysue.

Lee jerked around when she put a hand on his arm,
and she saw the panicked concern in his eyes. And the
angry frustration born of helplessness.

She gave him a quick smile and hurried up to the
counter, where she waited almost a full minute before
one of the nurses looked up and asked what she wanted.
When Jennifer asked her about Marysue, the woman
nodded.

"Just came in, you're right," she said, tapping a long
finger on a pile of papers beside her keyboard. "I'm afraid
you can't see her now, though, dear. One of the doctors
is with her."

"Do you know if she's—"

The woman shook her head. "I have no idea. Now,
please, sit down. There's a lot to do. You'll find out soon
enough."

Lee opened his mouth to protest, but Jennifer hushed him with a look. She knew it was fruitless trying to argue, especially when another ambulance pulled up and the area exploded into sudden activity. She pulled him out of the way toward the waiting area on the right and made him sit on one of the plastic chairs. She stood for a moment herself, watching the personnel bustling around the new casualty, then dropped into her chair and folded her hands in her lap.

By looking to her right she could see down the corridor to the examining rooms that opened off it. The injured waiting until dispositions could be made for each of their cases.

"She's going to be all right," Lee said flatly, staring at the stretcher being wheeled into the far hall.

"I know," she said and prayed that it was true.

"She was right behind us. It isn't like she was in the back where the fire was."

She nodded.

She listened to the telephones ringing, the nurses talking among themselves about the fire; she heard someone moaning in one of the rooms. She saw people moving about, then no one at all as calm returned for the moment.

Then she felt rather than saw Lee shudder, and she looked at him quickly.

"You know," he said, finally meeting her gaze, "it sure hasn't been dull around here since I met you."

She wanted to laugh; she wanted to cry; she threw her arms around his neck and planted a solid kiss on his cheek.

"Hey," he said, his face coloring.

She was about to kiss him again when his expression changed, and she turned, just in time to see Conrad walking toward the exit, hands deep in his jacket pockets. He didn't notice them until Lee spoke his name, then he turned and sat with a loud sigh on the other side of Lee.

"Well?" Jennifer asked.

"She's all right," he said, swallowing hard and glancing away for a moment. "Smoke inhalation, that's all. She says she tripped over a stool and fell, someone ran over her back, and it took her awhile to get back up again." He scowled. "If I ever find out who did it. . ."

"Thank heavens," Lee said, slumping back in his seat.

"Where is she?" Jennifer asked.

"She has to stay overnight for observation. And she says to tell you that you're going to have think of a costume for her because she's"—he stopped and suddenly grinned, raising the pitch of his voice and speaking in a southern drawl—"she's recovering, child, from a horrid trauma and she depends on you to be sure she doesn't disgrace herself at the dance."

It was relief more than the words themselves that made them all laugh until the tears came; and they were still giggling when they stumbled into the night, oblivious to the puzzled looks others gave them.

It wasn't until they had reached the main street again that Conrad said, "I heard something. In the ambulance."

They watched him, saying nothing.

"The fire," he said. "One of the guys said the cops are pretty sure it was arson."

Six

JENNIFER AND LEE SAT IN THE DARK IN MARYSUE'S Thunderbird with the engine off, listening to the tick of the motor as it cooled.

The acrid stench of smoke still clung to their clothes and skin, and Jennifer could still smell the hospital, and she had a slow-growing fear that she was unable to shake.

Neither she nor Lee said anything right after Conrad had made his announcement about the possibility of arson, but once the shock had passed they spent nearly a half hour speculating on possible culprits. Most of the time they kidded, figuring it was someone who didn't like the food. But behind all the good-natured speculation was a very real possibility whose name none of them would speak out loud.

Lee, with characteristic stubbornness, finally decided that he had been right all along.

It had to have been a grease fire that had simply gotten out of hand. Jennifer and Zucco, however, disagreed, reminding him of the terrific explosion that had taken place.

By the time they had finished their friendly argument they were back at the Hilltop. Only one fire truck was left, and two police cruisers. The sawhorse barricades were gone. Two men in civilian clothes were sweeping broken glass into the gutter. Most of the onlookers had left, and it didn't require much effort to get one of the remaining policemen to let them retrieve Marysue's car. Marysue had given her keys to Conrad and told him to drive Jennifer home in her car. She hadn't wanted to leave the Thunderbird on the street in Staines overnight.

They decided that Lee would drive Jennifer home with Conrad following in his mother's car, so he could drive them back to town. Lee grinned and familiarized himself with the way in which the old car's equipment was arranged. Then he took off with the wheels squealing.

Jennifer's lungs still felt as if they were filled with smoke, and even as she sat in the car in front of her dorm she succumbed to a brief fit of harsh coughing.

And when it was done, she still didn't move.

She stared at the curve of the drive, at the globed lights around its rim, and couldn't help but remember the van as it accelerated away from the curb, charging directly at her. She shivered. And shivered again when she imagined the van being replaced by a fire ball.

Lee reached over and put his arm around her. As if coming out of a dream, she shook her head and smiled at him.

"Sleep on it," he told her, knowing what she'd been thinking about. She got out of the car, waved good-bye, and slipped up the steps to the porch. She paused on the porch to turn and wave good-bye again to Lee before he drove off to park Marysue's car.

A look around the crescent to the left.

The dean's house was dark.

Don't do it, she ordered herself then. Use your head for once.

A brief smile, and she glanced down at her watch and was surprised that it was only nine-thirty; she had been gone a little more than three hours, yet it seemed as if she had been in town all night. She hurried over the thresh-hold and into the foyer.

"Hey, Field!" she heard as she passed the common room.

She looked in and saw the Visran twins at one of the card tables, a two-handed game of solitaire spread out before them. She waved and walked in, waved to another group who looked away from the television just long enough to greet her, and pulled up a chair.

"Jen," said Amy, her hair in pigtails, "you look terrible."

"Thanks," she muttered.

"Were you at the fire?" Marty asked, glaring at her sister. Jennifer nodded. "We heard about it."

Jennifer sat up. "Really?"

"Sure," and she jerked a thumb over her shoulder. "Pie had her radio on, of course. Biggest news since World War II, if you believe the local news folks. It got her mad. The bulletin interrupted her game."

Craning her neck, Jennifer spotted an overweight girl in coveralls watching a show on TV while, at the same time, listening to a radio with an earplug. She wasn't surprised. Marylinn Zonchek, known as Pie because of her weakness for virtually anything with a crust, was a fanatical sports fan and was reputed to have never missed a single game of the Celtics, the Red Sox, or the Bruins. The way she was grunting and twisting now, Jennifer figured it was football she was listening to right then.

"Was it really bad?" Amy asked contritely. "Some of the kids went into town, but they haven't come back yet."

"Bad enough," she said and told them the story. By the time she was done, the rest of the girls had come over, and she was touched that their primary concern was

Marysue's condition. They were all relieved that Marysue would be back in the morning. And once the question of her condition was taken care of, the air was filled with reasons why anyone would want to set fire to the Hilltop. The concern then was that the fire had effectively removed the only reasonably decent place in Staines to hang out.

It didn't take long before Jennifer was nearly forgotten, and she wasn't disappointed. An overwhelming weariness had suddenly overtaken her, and she wanted nothing more than to get cleaned up and ready to crawl into a nice warm bed.

She started for the stairs, paused in the foyer to listen to the others, and shook her head. She was just unlocking her room when she heard someone behind her. She turned and saw Pie walking toward her, earplug dangling over her shoulder, a tiny radio clasped in her hand.

"You sure do have your fun, don't you, Field," she said, her perpetually flushed face creased in a disdainful sneer.

"I get around," Jennifer said, opening the door.

"Yeah. Well, try to stay out of trouble, huh? You're giving the school a bad name."

Jennifer gaped at her, watching her broad back as she moved on down the hall. But she didn't say anything. Pie was not the best-liked young woman in the school, and as a senior she had become downright insufferable. There were some rumors that she had been accepted already at Stanford and others that her father had spread enough money around to get her into West Point if she wanted.

It was clear that Pie thought Jennifer was totally out of her element at Thaler.

"Hey, Field, what are you looking at!" the girl demanded from the far corner.

Jennifer blinked and passed a hand over her face, not realizing she had been staring. "Nothing," she called back. "Just thinking, that's all."

Pie nodded. "Sine. Well, think about this—the dean was around before. Looking for you. Someone told him you were in town with Beauford." Her smile was quick and mirthless. "Guess you're in it again, huh?"

And she vanished around the corner.

For just a second Jennifer wanted to chase after her, to find out exactly what Dramon had said. But that moment passed and she pushed into her room, closing the door behind her. She leaned against it and stared at the night-black windows.

So he really is back, she thought.

He was back, and he was looking for her.

"Just stay put, Jen," Lee told her. "Don't do anything stupid."

She was back downstairs, using the public telephone. There were very few kids in the common room then—it was well past ten. She had taken a chance calling him. Luckily he had answered on the first ring, almost as if he'd been waiting for her.

"But, Lee," she said, cupping the mouthpiece with one hand, "if he was looking for me— "

"Don't even think it," he interrupted.

"But the van, the fire—what if there really is a connection?"

"And what if there isn't?"

She shook her head. "He was looking for me."

A pause, and she could hear a radio playing somewhere in his house.

"All right," he said at last. "We might as well assume the worst, okay? Will that make you happy?"

"Lee, I don't understand you," she protested. "It doesn't take a genius to figure out he's not going to be pleased to see any of us again."

"And he's no idiot, remember?" he said. "You're saying he's trying to kill you."

"Not just me, I don't think," she said quietly.

There was a long silence before he said, "Look, I'll be on campus tomorrow afternoon. Please, *please* don't do anything until we can talk, okay? Jen—just be cool."

And then she understood his curious reluctance, the lack of his usual temper—he was afraid for her. He was afraid she would do something that he couldn't help her with. He was afraid she would get hurt.

"All right, I promise," she said then. "Can I brush my teeth?"

"You can't even breathe," he answered, relief clear in his voice. "Just wait."

She made a second call.

"Jenny," Conrad said, "what about Marysue?"

"What about her? You told me she was okay, and you're going to pick her up in the morning."

"But if you're right, she's down there tonight all alone. Anything could happen to her!"

She cursed herself then for calling him. She had never seen him as upset as he had been that night, and now all she was doing was feeding his worries about Marysue. He was completely ignoring the warning she had given him.

"Nothing's going to happen," she assured him firmly. "He's not unknown in town, remember? He's not going to walk right in and do something to her."

"He could disguise himself."

"Zucco, will you please calm down? You're not going to help her acting like this." She frowned. "Zucco?" There was silence. "Conrad, are you there?"

The dial tone burred in her ear then, and when she called his number again, and once again after that, she heard nothing but a busy signal. She hung up, stared at the receiver, then slapped herself lightly on the forehead.

"And you were going to think first, remember?"

But there was nothing she could do.

Conrad was either going to stay home or go to the hospital, and she was in no position to stop him. Lee was right. What she had to do was get some rest and wait until they were all together before deciding anything.

Halfway up the stairs she told herself that again.

In her room, with her bathrobe wrapped snugly around her, she suggested to her shadow that it quit looking at her as if it knew what she was going to do before she even did it.

In the shower, with the warm water pounding over her head, she closed her eyes and tried to think about what she was going to wear to the dance on Friday night.

And back in her room she stared at her nightgown, looked at the open door to the closet, and groaned out loud.

"You are impossible, Field," she said as she dressed.

But she knew herself too well.

No matter what Lee had said, nothing short of a hundred pills was going to give her any sleep that night.

She checked her watch again and decided to wait until the dorm was quiet, everyone in her room studying or in bed asleep. In the meantime, she told herself not to go without thinking it through. She had to devise a plan.

And give herself a time limit so she wouldn't be tempted to stay too long.

She winced when she yawned and her jaw popped. She sat at her desk and pulled a sheet of notepaper toward her, picked up a pencil, and began doodling.

An hour passed.

There were still voices in the hall.

She threw the paper away and started on another.

When she next looked at the time it was almost midnight, and there was still a group of girls in the hall, laughing quietly. She was tempted to go to the door and make a fuss, but knew it would be useless. The fire was news, and there was nothing she'd be able to do to hurry them along.

She had to wait.

Even if it took most of the night.

Seven

THE CAMPUS WAS DESERTED.

There was no moon, and the stars were hidden behind a black layer of cloud.

The house—Dramon's house—was cold, the deep, lifeless cold of open graves and empty tombs, the cold of an old and crumbling place that has been empty for decades.

The house was large, ceilings hidden in shadow, corners too distant to mark the ends of walls, doorways arched high to allow the passage of dark giants.

And the house was dark, made darker by tiny flares of silver light that occasionally burst around the window coverings.

Floorboards creaked. The muffled grumbling of the furnace. The wind soughing across the canted mouth of the chimney. A branch of a dead bush scraping like a fingernail against a window pane— once, twice, once again.

The hum of the refrigerator as Jennifer finally allowed herself to breathe and begin to move across the kitchen's linoleum floor.

She had a penlight in her hand, and its narrow beam stabbed nervously at the walls and the doorways and led her into a narrow hall that brought her to the front foyer. She paused at the foot of the long, curving staircase that vanished overhead, covered the beam with one hand, and listened.

There was nothing but the house, talking to itself.

The cold air was slightly stale, smelling as if the house had been sealed off against intrusion.

And still she listened, until she was positive no one knew she was there.

Then she exposed the light again and started to check the first floor.

The massive, shadow-lined living room was filled with elegant, eighteenth-century Chippendale furniture— each piece made huge as the small light illuminated it and cast its shadow across the walls.

In the dining room, below the crystal chandelier there was a large mahogany table with matching side chairs. A thin layer of dust covered the table and felt like grit when she ran a finger across it.

Aiming the light up the stairs, she forced her hand not to tremble. She saw nothing but the black absorbing the white light, as if a veil had been drawn across it, as if someone were up there, watching.

And waiting.

Impatiently she pushed a hair out of her eyes.

A draught swirled across the floor, curling cold around her ankles.

With a shiver she moved to the side of the staircase, examining the intricate paneling beneath the banister until, with a slight widening of her eyes, she saw a door in the paneling. A glance left and right, and she took hold of the latch.

And something moved upstairs.

She held her breath.

There was silence.

At first she thought it was only the wind gently nudging the house toward dawn, but when the sound came again, she knew what it was—someone, or something, was walking along a carpeted hall, toward the stairs.

Quickly she switched off her flashlight and opened the door, ducked in, and closed it again. Then she turned the light back on and saw that she was standing at the head of a wooden staircase leading to the cellar.

Above her someone was starting down to the foyer. Slowly. One careful step at a time.

Her eyes closed briefly before she headed down into the basement. She grimaced at each sound she made, sure she was being heard on the other side of the door. But no one challenged her, nothing sprang out of the dark at her, and when she reached the bottom, she paused for a moment.

The floor was concrete.

The walls were made of stone.

To her right the penlight picked out the massive bulk of the furnace.

To her left were the stairs leading up and to the outside.

Behind her the door at the top of the stairs creaked. Someone was coming down.

She gasped. A quick scramble to her left for the safety of the out-of-doors. Five quick steps up and then the cellar door overhead. It wouldn't budge. She pushed up with her shoulders and the door gave slightly as the sound on the wooden treads seemed to increase.

He was coming closer.

One last shove and an outside view of the nightsky was her reward.

Her mouth open, her eyes wide, one arm in front of her face for protection, she propelled herself into the night.

And it was several long, frightening seconds before she realized she was safe.

A sprint behind the buildings to her dorm. Up the fire stairs. A quick look and her room.

Sagging back in one of her armchairs, she gulped for air and rubbed at her eyes. There were beads of perspiration along her brow, and her back was stiff. Her vision was still somewhat blurred, and it took several tries before she was able to read her watch. She realized with a groan that it was already nearly three. Four hours until she had to get up.

"You're something else," Jennifer muttered to herself as she stretched out on her bed and fell into a sound sleep.

Yet, as she got ready for her first class and prayed that she'd be able to stay awake through it, it wasn't hard for her to figure out that Dramon hadn't really been in the house the night before, because he'd never have let her go. Her fear had stimulated her imagination.

It would serve as a warning—that attempting to beard the lion in his den wasn't something she ought to do alone again, no matter how urgent she felt the need.

She decided not to tell Lee about her adventure. That afternoon they could work out a plan.

There was a message for her taped to the wall beside the telephone in the common room; Conrad had called from the hospital to tell her that Marysue was being kept for another day, for further observation.

She called the number scribbled on the bottom of the paper and was put on hold by the hospital operator. After nearly five minutes she gave up and tried the Changs' house. No one answered there, either. She would have to wait and talk to him later.

On her way to class she ducked into the dining hall and grabbed a couple of rolls from a tray near the door. Marty Visran told her she looked as if she'd slept in her clothes all night; Jennifer only grunted.

She dozed off twice in her first class, and as soon as it was dismissed, she hurried to the Union to try to call the hospital again. The moment she was put on hold, she hung up.

Good thing it's not an emergency, she thought as she moved on to her next class and dozed off again, providing sadistic delight to her classmates when the instructor dropped a heavy book on her desk to wake her up.

"You could always go as Rip Van Winkle," Amy said after class.

"What?"

"You know, the guy that slept for twenty years?"

"Very funny."

Since her next class wasn't until after lunch, and Lee wouldn't be on campus until two, she returned to her room and threw herself onto her bed. And dozed on and off for the next hour, slipping in and out of dreams that made no sense.

And when at last she could sleep no longer, she pushed herself to her feet and stared in the mirror. Marty was right—she did look awful, and she spent ten minutes trying to cover the circles under her eyes. She changed her clothes, brushed her hair, and tossed the hairbrush onto the bed when she heard a familiar voice laughing in the hall.

She yanked the door open just as Pie Zonchek passed, then reached out and tapped the girl on the shoulder.

Pie turned, saw who it was, and rolled her eyes. "What do you want, Field?"

"Did you really see the dean last night?"

The fat girl's eyes narrowed. "What's it to you?"

"But you said—"

"I said I heard, that's all." Then she looked startled, an expression that lasted only a fraction of a second. "You mean you haven't gone to his office yet? Oh, brother, Field, you really are asking for it."

Jennifer ignored the sneer in her voice. She was puzzled by Pie's startled look, as if the girl were momentarily afraid. "Who told you he was looking for me?"

"How should I know? It's all over campus."

She saw the fear now in Pie as her gaze shifted and her hands continued to move. Jennifer leaned against the jamb. "No. No, it's not."

Pie's face flushed. "You calling me a liar, Field?"

"I don't know. Are you?"

The girl took a step toward her.

"I mean," Jennifer said blandly, "if it's all over campus why hasn't anyone else told me about it?"

Pie stopped. "How should I know?"

Jennifer shrugged. "You tell me, Pie."

Zonchek stared at her and stiffened abruptly. "I don't have to listen to you, Field," she snapped, walking away. "I told you what I had to tell you and that's all that matters."

For a second Jennifer considered dropping the subject, then changed her mind and ran after Pie, catching up just at the shower room. She grabbed Pie's shoulder and, using more surprise than strength, pushed her into the shower room. Pie tried to get out, but Jennifer shoved her back again.

"I'll mangle you, Field," Zonchek warned.

"Okay."

She knew she was taking a big risk. Zonchek was slightly taller, outweighed her by almost a hundred pounds, and probably could swat her aside as if she were nothing more than a fly. But Jennifer had to know if Pie was lying. And if she was, why.

Zonchek glanced from side to side nervously, took a step toward her, and raised a meaty fist. "Move," she said.

Jennifer shook her head.

"Field," Pie warned.

"Just tell me," she said. "And I'll be on my way."

Suddenly the color faded from Pie's cheeks, and her eyes lost their expression of bravado. Her mouth opened, closed, and she turned to face the row of tiled shower stalls.

"Pie, for crying out loud, what's the big deal?"

The girl turned suddenly and pushed Jennifer aside, ran into the hall and up toward the front. Jennifer didn't chase her; she knew then that Pie had lied about "hearing" that the dean wanted her, about the whole campus knowing the man wanted to see her. She distinctly remembered the girl telling her that Dramon was around the dorm, looking for her.

If it were an ordinary summons regarding school or her work, she would have to go to his office. And if it wasn't, why would Zonchek want her there? Unless —unless she was told to make sure Jennifer got there.

By whom?

For that there had to be only one answer.

Eight

THERE WAS NO QUESTION OF HER ATTENDING THE rest of her classes. She had to get in touch with the others as fast as she could and tell them what had happened. She tried phoning but no one answered at Conrad's or Lee's.

She ran back to her room, grabbed her coat and gloves and, taking a deep breath, took the extra set of car keys that she kept for Marysue. She ran down the stairs two at a time. Pie wasn't in the common room, and Jennifer didn't see her when she got outside and trotted to the parking lot. Pie had been given instructions and was clearly afraid because Jennifer hadn't done what she should have.

Jennifer needed no other proof that the dean was really back.

Jennifer had never driven before, but her situation was desperate. She had watched her friends drive often and knew she'd be able to manage.

The Thunderbird started on the third try, and Jennifer drove very slowly around the drive, trying to get a feel for steering. The large car shuddered, leaped forward, and stalled. Jennifer started it again and concentrated on keeping the vehicle on the road.

She continued down into the valley, driving fifteen miles an hour, constantly stalling and restarting the car. Once she had to pull over to the side to wipe the perspiration from the palms of her hands.

Only when the road leveled and straightened did she begin to relax. When she approached Conrad's house, she noticed there was no car in the driveway and drove on, impatiently tapping the steering wheel when it seemed as if she was going to get caught by every red light in town.

At the hospital she wasted fifteen minutes trying to find a parking space large enough for her to pull into. She finally ended up two blocks away. By the time she reached the reception desk she was panting, and the smile she used for the pink-coated woman behind the counter was strained.

"Marysue Beauford," she said.

Thinking: C'mon, lady, c'mon!

The woman, apparently sensing her impatience, calmly adjusted a pair of half glasses and searched through the visitor's pass file, missing the name twice. Jennifer could stand it no longer and leaned over and tapped the correct card. The woman nodded, took her time pulling it, and handed it over. Jennifer hurried to the elevator bank and paced in front of it until she was able to get on one that wasn't filled with medical personnel coming from the labs one floor below.

On the second floor she followed a yellow line painted on the wall until she reached an intersection of four corridors, with a nurse's station in the center. None of the women looked up; none asked her if she needed help.

A glance at the card to be sure of the room number, and she tried not to run.

There were two beds in the semiprivate room. The one nearest the door was obviously unoccupied; the one near the window was rumpled.

But Marysue wasn't in it.

She stepped back into the hall to be sure she had the right number, then stepped in again and looked around carefully while she tried to slow her breathing. The closet was empty. When she knocked on the bathroom door and received no reply, she opened it and looked in—it was empty.

All right, she told herself as she left. All right, there's a perfectly good explanation, right? Nothing's wrong. Beauford's okay. There's nothing to worry about.

The nurse's station was busy, and it took her awhile before she was able to get someone's attention.

"Marysue Beauford," she said, holding out the visitor's card for the nurse to see. "I came to see her, but she's not in her room. Nobody's there."

The woman sighed loudly and flicked invisible lint from her starched whites. "Y'know," she said, "I swear those people down at reception would lose their heads if they weren't screwed on."

"What do you mean?"

"Beauford. Smoke inhalation from the fire, right?"

"Yes, yes."

"She's gone."

Jennifer stared stupidly at the card, stared back at the nurse. "But she can't be! I got a message only this morning—"

"Young lady," the nurse said stiffly, "I think I ought to know when one of my patients is gone, don't you? And this Marysue Beauford is gone."

"But—"

The distress on her face softened the woman's attitude, and the nurse held up a finger, a signal to wait. Jennifer watched her confer with someone else at the station, then turned around and looked back the way she had come.

Gone.

How could she be gone?

Then, abruptly, she sagged against the counter with explosive relief. Conrad, of course. They had let her go. Conrad had been there and he took her home or out to get something to eat. Or something. She turned back then when she realized the nurse was talking to her.

"I'm sorry," she said. "What did you say?"

"It was her father," the woman told her, scanning a sheet of green paper she was holding. "I remember him now. He came in, talked with the doctor, and took her home. There was no reason for her to stay, you see."

Jennifer shut her eyes and lowered her head for a moment. "She's from Virginia," she said at last, her voice not sounding like her own. "Her father—"

"A very handsome man, isn't he?" the nurse interrupted. "Darkest eyes I've ever seen. Actually, he kind of gave me the shivers, you know what I mean? It was like he was looking right through me."

"Did she go with him willingly?" Jennifer asked.

"Well, of course, he was her father, wasn't he?"

"When?" Jennifer whispered.

The nurse shrugged. "About an hour ago. As I said, he was taking her home."

Jennifer backed away slowly, turned, and stared blindly at the elevators.

Then she bolted for the fire stairs before the nurse could stop her.

Dramon has her.

She sat in the Thunderbird and shook.

Dramon has Marysue.

The keys fell from her hand when she tried to start the ignition. A second try failed as well, and she had to steady her right hand with her left. It was enough to start the engine. Then she pulled out into the street and drove slowly toward the center of town. She had to get Lee. He wouldn't have left yet for Thaler. She hoped he was having lunch at home after his morning classes at Staines High School. Lee would help her. Lee would know what to do.

Dramon.

Breathe deep, she ordered then when she felt the tears threaten to rise. In and out, breathe deep.

As soon as she saw a parking space in the center of town, she pulled into it, driving over the curb. Quickly she shut off the engine, leaned back and swallowed, and winced when she realized she had been biting on the inside of her cheek.

Only then did she look across the street at the front of Fawkes Hardware, and she gasped.

Oh, no, she thought. Oh, no. Now what?

As if in a trance she walked across the street, paying no attention to the car that blared its horn at her, to its squealing brakes, and to the shouts from the angry driver who ordered her out of the way.

There were two men working in front of the shop, pulling out jagged splinters of broken glass from the display window's aluminum frame. A scaffold had been erected, a danger sign planted on the sidewalk, and she gaped at it all as she stumbled inside, ignoring the Closed sign hanging on the door.

There was no one there.

The aisles were empty, the back counter was unmanned, and when she knocked on the door that led to the storeroom in back, no one answered.

"Lee?" she called.

The sound of glass shattering.

"Mr. Fawkes?"

One of the workmen swore, and the other one hushed him up.

"Lee, it's Jenny!"

No answer.

The storeroom door was locked.

She pushed a hand through her hair, hurried back to the street, and asked one of the workmen if he knew where Mr. Fawkes was. He told her the place was closed, the family probably at home. Jennifer stepped away from the shop and looked up at the windows on the building's second floor, where Lee and his parents lived.

The blinds were down, the windows closed.

There was a door between the hardware store and a boutique on the left. She had never been upstairs before, and despite the urgency she felt, she was nervous about going in, more so when she saw the narrow staircase that led up to a small landing.

He's gonna kill me, she thought for no reason at all. He's gonna kill me.

Behind the freshly painted door at the top, she could hear a radio playing softly. After drying her palms on her jeans, she rang the bell and stepped back, stiffening when the radio was shut off and footsteps approached.

"Well," the man said who opened the door, "you must be Jen."

She nodded jerkily.

He was short, stocky, and very nearly bald. He was wearing a white shirt whose sleeves were carefully rolled above the elbows, faded jeans, and an incongruous pair of red plaid suspenders.

"Well," said Andrew Fawkes, stepping aside with a friendly smile, "you'd better come in. Lee'll shoot me if I keep you standing out here all day."

She found herself in a comfortable living room, much larger than she would have expected from the windows outside, and filled with furniture that looked as if it belonged in a home, not in a showroom.

"Mr. Fawkes," she said, feeling suddenly uneasy, "I—I was downstairs and I saw—what happened?"

Lee's father frowned. "You didn't get my message?"

"No. I—"

"Early this morning," he said, his face darkening with anger, "Lee was helping me set up a new display in the window before he went to school. I really don't know exactly what went on because it happened so fast, but—"

She wanted to scream; she waited instead.

"Someone—I don't know if it was more than one—threw a couple of bricks through the window. One of them, and some glass, hit Lee."

"Oh, no," she whispered and sat down heavily in the nearest chair.

Mr. Fawkes, realizing he had broken the news a little bluntly, hurried over and took her hands. "He's all right," he assured her. "A quick trip to the emergency room, a few stitches, and he'll be right as rain in a couple of days."

"But who did it?" she asked.

"I don't know. I was more worried about Lee. And by the time I thought to go outside to see if I could catch them, the street was empty. It was early. About seven or so."

She looked down at the hands gently engulfing hers, and she squeezed them. "Can I see him?"

"If I didn't let you, I'd have a very angry son on my hands."

She grinned and followed him down a short hall to a closed door. He knocked, winked at her, and opened the door.

"Company," he said and waved her in.

"Company?" Lee said from his bed. "C'mon, Dad, I don't want to see—holy—"

"Language, boy!" Mr. Fawkes cautioned with a smile. "There's a lady present."

Lee's face was red from medication, and a line of stitches was traced across his left cheek. His right eye, however, was what Jennifer couldn't help staring at— it was covered by a white bandage wrapped slanted around his head.

"Lee," she said softly, and after Mr. Fawkes nudged her, hurried over to sit on the edge of the mattress. Her hand went out to touch the bandage, and Lee grabbed her wrist and shook his head.

"Smarts," he said.

"Your eye!"

"No," said Mr. Fawkes, still standing in the door-way. "It was, thankfully, untouched. But there's a pretty nasty cut just underneath it, and a bump the size of Mount Everest by his temple. He's lucky he wasn't blinded."

"It isn't that bad," Lee muttered, clearly embarrassed at having Jennifer in his room. "I'll live."

"You know you will," his father said. "I can't run that store by myself. I'm too old."

There was a monient of awkward silence then, until Mr. Fawkes mumbled something about the kitchen and left. And once he was gone, Lee grabbed her arms and pulled her to him, kissed her once, hard, and tenderly eased her away.

"Pirate," he said.

Puzzled, she frowned.

"I'll have to go as a pirate. Jesse James didn't wear an eye patch."

"Are you really all right?" she demanded, wondering how much more she would have to face that day before she cracked.

"Yeah," he said. "Like my dad says, eight stitches, a few cuts, and a heck of a bump. I've got a headache you won't believe, but the doc gave me some pills. I'll be all right." He looked at her until she nodded her belief, then closed his eyes as a lance of pain made him grunt. When he opened his eyes again, he raised an eyebrow. "You're really here."

"Sure."

"But why?"

She had almost forgotten, seeing Lee helpless like that, and quickly decided that she wouldn't say anything. He didn't need any more worries; he had to get well.

"Your father left a message for me at the school," she said. "So I came right away."

Only half a lie, she thought.

And she managed to deflect any more questions, insisting that he rest while she told him about her morning and how she'd fallen asleep in her classes. The visit lasted only ten minutes, however, because Mr. Fawkes returned and suggested that his son needed to rest.

Lee protested, but weakly. Jennifer took courage in hand and kissed his cheek before leaving. At the door Lee's father thanked her for coming and told her that she'd be welcome to return for supper. She promised that she would and hurried down the steps.

The workmen were still repairing the window.

But when she looked across the street, the Thunderbird was gone.

Nine

JENNIFER CAREFULLY SCANNED THE PARKING SPACES across the street. In her excitement she must have missed it; a car like that wouldn't just disappear.

But it was gone.

She raked a hand through her hair.

A passing truck backfired, and she scarcely heard it.

Her first reaction was to ask the workmen if they had seen anything, spotted anyone hanging around the Thunderbird, but they shook their heads without speaking. They had been too busy preparing the frame for the new window. And there was no one else on the street to ask.

For the second time that day she walked across the street without paying attention to traffic, and just as she reached the other side a station wagon pulled into the space where Marysue's car had been. She stared at it for several seconds before moving away, walking slowly, watching every car that passed her, looking up every side street. She knew she was close to breaking down. She could feel it. The tears were poised, ready to fall.

Who? she wondered. Who had done it?

She knew she should go to the police, but she dismissed the thought immediately. What if they asked to see her driver's license? What she needed was a friendly face right then.

Conrad. She needed Conrad.

And the moment his name came to mind, she began to run, feeling the cold air slap and snap against her cheeks.

Conrad would know what to do.

She had been through too much already that day, and she didn't want to think anymore, didn't want to make any decisions. Let Conrad do it. Let him think of a way to get Marysue back, find the car, and do something about Dramon.

She stumbled into a couple coming out of a store, called back an apology, and ran on.

She was tired.

Suddenly and inexplicably, the surge of energy she had felt after discovering Beauford missing had left her, leaving her feeling drained, hollow, and not quite resigned, but too weary to act.

The stolen Thunderbird had been the last straw—she was tired of fighting when the fighting was supposed to be over.

A small dog chased her for nearly a full block, barking joyfully, playfully snapping at her heels. She paid it no heed. She was almost completely numb.

By the time she had left the business district behind, she slowed to a stumbling half trot, half walk. Her lungs were protesting the blades of icy air she took in, her eyes were watering from the wind she made by walking quickly. She heard nothing but the dull slap of her feet on the pavement and the ragged hoarseness of her own breathing. And she didn't look around when a car honked at her several times.

Conrad, she prayed. Conrad, please be home.

The car honked again.

Thinking it was a guy trying to pick her up, she scowled and looked away and nearly tripped over a tricycle left on the sidewalk. She glanced up and saw the red Thunderbird crawling along the curb. By the time she had twisted and stumbled past the little bike, her mouth had dropped open in astonishment. And snapped closed when she saw Conrad behind the wheel, leaning over the seat, and beckoning to her urgently.

"Why?" she demanded when she slid inside and slammed the door.

"I still have the keys from last night," Conrad said. "And I want to give Marysue a scare."

Jennifer wanted to laugh with relief, but all that came out were a bitter, short bark and a harsh spate of coughing when all the words she wanted to say became jammed in her throat. Conrad waited, tapping the wheel hard with the heel of one hand. Keeping her gaze on the street ahead, Jennifer was able to get the whole story out, from Pie's deception to Lee's so-called accident.

"But why didn't you go get her this morning?" Jennifer asked.

"I was going to go over at ten to spring her. But I got a message at school that she had been discharged."

Conrad paused. "Do you have any idea where she is now?" he asked quietly.

Until that moment she hadn't.

At the question, however, she nodded. "Where else? At school. At *his* place. The house."

"All right, then," he said, pulling away from the curb. "Then we go get her."

"Just like that?"

"Just like that."

Jennifer did not protest. She knew it was a bad idea, and knew, too, there was no question but that it had to be some kind of trap. Dramon's bold move at the hospital had all the earmarks of taunting bait. He had to have known that one of them, Conrad or her, would recognize the nurse's description of Marysue's bogus father, and he would be counting on them to charge headlong to the rescue.

And the moment they stepped into the house, the trap would close around them.

The car sped up as the town was left behind, and its engine labored up the hill toward Thaler. Shadows dappled the blacktop, and a quartet of crows wheeled in slow circles over the trees.

Conrad's expression was grim and determined, yet Jennifer had to tell him what she thought.

It didn't make any difference.

"But what I don't get," he said, "is how he did it. He just walked in and out like that? I mean, the man isn't exactly an unknown in this town, you know."

It took her only a few seconds to find the answer—if the aliens had been able to disguise themselves as humans, it wasn't so hard to imagine that Dramon knew or had learned the same ability.

"It wouldn't take much," she said when he expressed his doubt. "You don't have to be completely made over. A small change here or there, even just a mustache, a hat, and a pair of glasses, and you can fool most people for a short time."

"Just long enough," he said tightly, "to take her out before anyone knew who he was."

"Yes."

And, she added silently, perhaps just long enough to try to run her down in a van, to throw a brick through a plate glass window.

Not much change, but just enough.

"But why did she go with him?" he asked then. "She'd recognize him. Why would she just leave with him like that?"

She shook her head helplessly. "I don't know, Zucco. I don't know. That's something we'll have to ask her."

Suddenly, as the road began to level out at the crown, she said, "Slow down."

Conrad frowned.

"Zucco, slow down! You can't go racing onto campus like this. It'll attract too much attention."

"You won't stop me," he said.

"I'm not trying to stop you," she said. "I just want to make sure we get there in one piece."

It was clear that he wanted to charge in, grab Marysue, and ride off again. But his foot did leave the accelerator. And finally, as they approached the entrance, he braked and drove almost sedately into the parking lot, where they sat for several minutes in silence.

"It's crazy," he said when they got out at last. "I don't get it."

"Neither do I," she admitted. "He's sure not trying to be sneaky or anything."

He nodded. "No kidding. So now what?"

She thought about how, only a few minutes before, she had been ready to let Conrad, or anyone else, do her thinking for her. But the look on his face, and the image of Lee lying helpless in bed, changed it.

It changed everything.

"Now," she said. "We do it now."

They moved carefully through the woods that surrounded the campus, keeping the three houses on their left. Though it was impossible to be completely silent,

Jennifer wanted to be sure they attracted no undue attention, which was why they were using the woods for cover.

And when they reached the back of the dean's house and were crouched behind a screen of shrubs, she scanned the windows for signs of anyone watching, staring at the curtains for movement, trying to peer through the reflections of the trees in the panes for hints that someone was aware that they were here.

There was nothing.

Though it was broad daylight, and though she could hear faint sounds of activity around the crescent, she had the distinct feeling that she and Zucco were alone.

She pointed to a plywood lean-to under which had been stacked a cord of roughly chopped wood. Conrad nodded when he realized what she wanted. Then, with a wink and a stiff smile, she walked boldly into the yard, reached into the shelter and grabbed a length of wood. Conrad followed and marched with her to the back door, moving quickly without running, holding his makeshift club at his side.

The door was unlocked, as it had been the night before.

Jennifer and Conrad wasted no time, but stepped into the linoleum-floored kitchen, the same large and airy room that Jennifer had invaded the night before. The refrigerator still humming softly in the corner.

With a finger to her lips, indicating that Conrad should remain quiet, Jennifer looked warily around the room as she breathed in deeply, twice, and turned wide-eyed to focus on Conrad.

"I know," Conrad whispered. "It's gas!" He ran to the stove and turned the unlit burners off as Jennifer began to open the kitchen windows.

She knew that the doorway directly ahead led into the short, carpeted hall that was paneled with gleaming dark wood. With no conscious concern for anything but opening windows, she plunged into the hallway, her body becoming rigid as she prepared herself for a blow she knew had to come. But the first floor of the house was completely silent, with no sound of anyone moving. It was free of danger other than that from the gas.

Unable to open the fixed front hall windows, she hefted the wooden club that she still held and broke the narrow panes into daggerlike shards.

"Who's up there? Jen, is that you? Conrad?" came Marysue's almost unintelligible voice from the cellar.

Marysue? It had to be. Jennifer rushed to the door built into the paneling under the staircase and groped for the curved latch painted to resemble the wood around it.

From downstairs Marysue's voice called out again. This time hysterically. "Don't open that door. Whatever you do, don't touch it."

Jennifer let go of the latch that she had just managed to find and stood frozen to the spot. Conrad ran in from the living room, where he had been opening windows, and joined Jennifer. She had to bat his hand away as he reached out for the latch.

"No, don't touch it. Marysue said."

"Marysue, why can't we open the door?" Conrad shouted.

"I don't know exactly, but I saw Dramon attaching something to it. Just trust me. Come around and then down through the cellar door."

Conrad and Jennifer looked at each other, not knowing if Marysue were an unwilling participant in a plan to lure them downstairs.

They nodded, knowing that they had to go to help her—no matter what.

They ran back through the kitchen to the outside, slowing only when they approached the bulkhead. They stood, silently looking down at the wooden rectangle leading to the cellar.

All right, Jennifer told herself. Do it, don't wait for an invitation.

The door lifted soundlessly, revealing the short, narrow flight of stairs. There was no light switch that she could find, but the basement windows were large enough and clean enough to give her sufficient light to see by.

With Conrad at her back, one hand lightly on her shoulder, she took the steps one at a time, slowly, wishing there were a banister to hold on to because her knees had become rubbery. The ragged length of wood she held grew heavy, and she shifted it to her other hand, wincing when a splinter dug into one finger.

On the bottom step she moved aside to let Conrad down first.

And Marysue's voice rang out, "Well, it certainly took you long enough."

Ten

MARYSUE WAS TIED BY CLOTHESLINE TO A LADDER-back chair next to the square, green furnace. She looked at them as if they were late picking her up for a party, but as soon as Conrad undid the knots binding her ankles and wrists, she moaned and burst into tears. He held her tightly, staring blindly over her shoulder at the stone wall.

Jennifer put her club down and signaled to Conrad that he should try to discover what Dramon had planned for them.

Conrad agreed and cautiously approached the inside wooden stairs. Slowly he felt his way up the treads, fingering each stair before setting his weight on it. Finally at the top he lightly ran his finger around the door frame.

"I have it," he said joylessly. "It's an ignition device, which would have produced a spark when we opened that door. With all that gas—Boom! We would have been blown away."

Marysue started to weep again—dramatically.

Jennifer, who had been standing next to her friend, bent down and asked solicitously, "Are you all right?"

"All right? You ask me if I'm all right?" Marysue's voice was pitched high, dangerously close to hysteria, and Conrad held her until the threat of hysteria had passed. "Of course I'm not all right, Field. I was abducted from my very own hospital bed, dragged out here, bound and gagged, tortured— "

"Tortured?" Conrad said angrily.

Marysue shrugged. "Well, maybe not tortured. And he didn't gag me either. But he did give me a shot to quiet me at the hospital so I'd go with him. *And* he was going to blow me up."

Jennifer looked at the stairs then and suggested they get out of there before the dean returned to see why the house hadn't exploded. The others agreed readily, and they left the way they'd come in, through the cellar door. They moved through the woods, angling around the campus's perimeter until they stepped out just ahead of the gymnasium building. Then, as though they were simply heading up the slope toward class or the dining hall, they walked three abreast, heads down, hands in pockets.

There was no sign of the dean.

"Shall we go to the dorm?" Marysue asked.

"No," Jennifer answered. "Conrad, remember?"

Conrad raised an eyebrow that brought him a gentle slap from Marysue, and they swung into the Student Union, turned right, and took a couch at the far corner of the lounge. The room was nearly filled— students gossiping, some trying halfheartedly to study, and a few standing in the doorway to the game room, shouting encouragement to what was obviously a vital game in the monthly table tennis tournament. The favorite was apparently winning.

"Tell us exactly what happened," Jennifer said, pleased at all the activity around her.

"Dramon walks in as sweet as you please, and that stupid nurse came in a couple of minutes later calling him my father, for pity's sake! She tells me to get dressed, and he just backs up and stands there in the door, looking at me. He just stands there!"

"Then why didn't you scream or say anything?" Zucco asked.

Marysue passed her hands over her face. "Because when he first came in, he walked over to me, stuck a needle with tranquilizers in my arm, and said something to me."

"What?"

" 'Jennifer.' "

Jennifer went cold.

"That's all he said?" Conrad asked, puzzled.

"That's all he had to Say," she replied. "If you could have seen the look on his face and heard the way he said it. . . ." She shuddered. "I thought he had you, Jen, or something. I wasn't thinking clearly with all the tranquilizers, so I just played the good little girl. He brought me back here, tied me up, and— "

"And you didn't call out or try to get away or anything?" Conrad scolded.

Marysue shrugged her shoulders. "I was drugged. I felt like I was walking through water. Besides, I didn't know what he meant when he said Jenny's name, remember? Maybe, if I'd tried something, he would have killed her."

Jennifer sat up and looked at Marysue, who immediately craned her neck to see how the game was going in the back room. Jennifer reached out and took Marysue's wrist, and a long second later Marysue looked back.

"What happened then?" Jennifer asked softly.

Beauford lowered her eyes.

"C'mon, Richmond, what did he say?"

The light in the front windows dimmed as the sun dropped toward the hills behind the academy; lights were turned on in the room and in the hall. The game ended to much cheering and laughter, and after a few minutes of whirlwind activity in the lounge, it emptied except for a pair of girls poring over an atlas.

Jennifer watched them enviously.

"He tied me up," Marysue said, lowering her voice because the noise had ended. "And then he stood over me. I thought it was the end. My little Virginia soul was about to depart, and the dumb thing is, all I could do was get angry. I was scared, but I was angry, too."

Jennifer nodded her understanding; Conrad held her hand more tightly.

"Then . . ." Marysue looked up at the ceiling and swallowed, hard. "Then he said he supposed my little friends would be along soon enough to save me. One of them, anyway, he hoped. He meant you, Jen."

Jennifer remembered Mr. Fawkes's invitation to dinner that night and wished there were some way she could make it. It would be safe there, in the Fawkes' apartment. Safe. And Lee would be with her.

"He wants you dead, Jen, and I don't think there's any-place you can hide. He'll try until he succeeds," Marysue finished in a rush and burst into tears again, burying her face against Conrad's chest.

Jennifer stood slowly, feeling a hundred years old and feeling nothing at all. She looked down at her friend, smiled at Conrad, and walked out of the room, out of the Union, and off the porch. She walked across the lawn, blinking at the nightwind, flexing her hands, and finally pulling her gloves from a pocket and slipping them on.

She didn't feel the cold as she headed for the pillars at the school's entrance.

She kept her mind deliberately blank until she was at the juncture of drive and highway, and then she stared at the shadowed slope of Ballad Hill across the way.

On the far side of that hill was where it all should have ended. On the far side was where the aliens had died.

But Dramon wasn't going to let it go.

It was her fault: that's what she guessed he was thinking. After all, she had been the one who had discovered the aliens' presence, and she who had unraveled their plot. And because of her it had failed. It made no difference to him that at the end she had had help, that she had never done it all herself.

Dramon—from the beginning—had focused on her.

And Dramon, at the end, wanted his revenge on her, not minding if others perished with her.

Footsteps running up behind her.

Conrad gasping her name as he staggered to a halt at her side.

She turned her head, then looked back at the hill.

"Jenny, Marysue and I've decided that you should come to my house tonight. We'll get my mother to call Rumbel, and he'll—"

"Do what?" she said quietly.

"Well, he's a cop," he said. "And he's on our side, right? He knows. He can help."

She shook her head. "No. I don't think so."

"But why?"

She looked squarely at him. "Zucco, he wants me, and nobody else. I don't know why, and I know that it doesn't make sense. Revenge doesn't make sense. If you bring anyone else into this, he'll back off. He'll be straight. He won't even jaywalk, for crying out loud."

Conrad opened his mouth to say "So?" and his eyes widened in understanding.

"I can't wait that long," she said. "I can't go home, I can't stay here, and I sure can't hide at your place. Sooner or later he's going to come for me." She shrugged. "Why not now?"

He wanted to argue, she could see it in his eyes, but he also knew that she had made up her mind and wouldn't budge. And he grinned.

"Okay," he said. "So here's the plan."

"Plan?" she echoed, almost laughing.

Just then the Thunderbird pulled up and Marysue leaned over to the passenger window. "Well?"

"No," he said.

"I knew it. She's a pain, Zucco. You don't know her like I do. She's a real pain."

"I think she's right."

"You're a pain too."

"Hey," Jennifer said. "Have I left the room without knowing it?"

"You've left your brain in your sock drawer, that's what you've done," Marysue told her, her voice harsh. "But as long as you're going to be dumb, you might as well have company."

"Oh," she said. "And that's the plan?"

"No," Zucco said, climbing into the car. "The plan is that Richmond drives me back to my place. I have a few things I want to pick up. Then she drives me back here, I stay in her room tonight, and I—"

"You do what?"

He grinned as the car rolled forward. "I'm guarding you."

"No!" she said, walking along beside the car. "No, that's not possible."

But he only saluted her, sat back, and waved Marysue on. And Jennifer could only watch as the automobile roared into the growing twilight and vanished around the bend. Then she started back for the dorm, feeling frustrated that they had taken on the responsibility for her safety without asking if she wanted their help and buoyant because they had done exactly that. She needed them, and they were there, and she hadn't had to ask.

The idea that Dramon was going to try to kill her was terrifying; but to sit back and let it happen was more terrifying still. That would mean handing over her life as if it meant nothing, to her or anyone else.

If he thought that, he was wrong.

The dorm was quiet.

She walked up the stairs and made her way to her room and stopped with her hand on the knob when Pie called her name.

"What?" she snapped without turning around.

A pudgy hand reached over her shoulder, a small envelope in it. "For you, Field," the girl said.

Jennifer took it and saw her name printed neatly on the face; then she opened her door, stepped in, and looked back at Pie, whose arrogant tone didn't match the frightened expression on her face.

"He scares you, doesn't he?" Jennifer said.

Pie, too startled to say anything, nodded once.

"He scares me, too." And she closed the door softly, leaned against it, and listened to Zonchek's footsteps rush away down the hall. Jennifer guessed Dramon had either told Pie some fanciful story which appealed to her snobbery or had threatened her with something— dismissal, failure, whatever—in order to get her to become his messenger.

It didn't matter.

She turned on the light, opened the envelope, and pulled out a stiff piece of paper.

An invitation.

"Miss Field, I will see you at the dance. Tomorrow."

There was no signature.

She didn't need one.

Eleven

WHEN NEITHER CONRAD NOR MARYSUE RETURNED within the hour, Jennifer went to the dining hall and ate alone. Or as alone as she could be with the Visran twins popping up every ten minutes to ask about her costume, someone else wanting to know about the English assignment, and someone else breaking into an arm-waving tirade about whales, dolphins, and helpless baby seals before thrusting a long petition into her hands and waiting there, hands on hips, until she signed it.

Midway through dessert, she was confronted by several members of the dance committee, who wanted her to be a judge of the best costume contest since, they had heard through the grapevine, she wasn't going to wear one.

A thought struck her and she started to smile. A hasty apology then, and a denial of the rumor, and she hurried through the last of her meal. She needed to think her idea through, but, she reasoned, there wasn't enough time. She ran out of the Union, looked in both directions, and finally saw the twins rounding the corner of the last dorm.

You're asking for it, Field, she told herself.

And she smiled, feeling reckless and somewhat giddy.

The twins, on the path down to the gymnasium, slowed but didn't stop when Jennifer called to them.

When she caught up, they greeted her in unison. And not for the first time she realized that the only way she could tell them apart was by Amy's pigtails. Without them, it would be like looking at a mirror.

"I have an idea," she said then.

Marty looked at her skeptically. "Beauford told me about your ideas, Field," she said. "I don't know if I want to hear it."

"It's about tomorrow night," she said.

Amy pulled thoughtfully on one of her pigtails. "What about it? You want to go as Little Red Riding Hood?"

She forced herself to laugh. "No, but there's a contest, right?"

They nodded.

"And you want to win, right?"

They nodded again, suspiciously.

"Then let me ask you a question—how long does it take to make one of your great costumes?"

I will see you at the dance.

She remembered then she had never called Lee's house. When she dialed Lee's father answered and readily accepted her apology for not making dinner. He told her that the meal hadn't turned out all that well anyway, and even his wife couldn't find a single kind word to say about it except that it was interesting. She laughed. He brought the telephone into Lee's room and, with a gentle admonition not to keep him on the line too long, handed it over.

"I've been thinking about the Halloween dance," she said after making sure that he was feeling at least no worse than before.

"Great," he said sourly. "I've blown the first chance I get all year to hobnob with the rich folk, and now you call to rub it in."

"I'm not rubbing it in."

"Well, it feels like it."

"Lee!" She glared at the receiver. "I don't have time for your silly pouting, okay?"

There was a pause.

"I'm not pouting."

"Okay."

"Well, I'm not."

"All right. So you're not pouting."

Then she heard him cover the mouthpiece while he laughed.

"Listen," she said then. "I have an idea, and I want you to tell me how stupid it is."

"Oh, no," he groaned.

She talked for nearly ten minutes, ordering him not to interrupt after he tried it once. Then she waited for his reply for nearly one full minute when she was finished. Finally she tapped a fingernail against the receiver.

"Lee, you still there?"

"Jenny, don't do it," he said.

"That doesn't tell me what you think."

"I think it's stupid."

"Yeah. I know."

"And it's dangerous."

"I know that too."

His voice became quiet. "Jen, it isn't going to work. I don't want you to do it."

"Lee, it's—"

Then he was stern and, at the same time, almost pleading. "Promise me you'll forget it, okay? Promise me you'll come here tomorrow and hold my hand. I hurt, Jen. I hurt bad. I—it would be nice to see you."

She swallowed against a sudden burr in her throat. "I can't, Lee," she whispered.

"You can't come, or you can't promise?"

Her eyes closed. "Both."

And she hung up before he could talk her out of it.

at the dance

Back in her room she sat at her desk and tried several times to write her parents a letter. But each time she launched into an explanation of what had been happening to her since she had arrived at Thaler, she tore the paper up and threw it away in frustration and disgust.

It was useless.

It wasn't something she could explain on paper; they had to see her face, her eyes, the way her hands moved, everything that would add force and conviction to her words. Writing it out wouldn't work.

She extinguished the lights then and stared out the window and watched the stars wink on, watched the moonlight outline the hills and blend them with shadows into one massive backdrop, one unassailable wall beyond which was a world that would never know what had happened at Thaler.

It was unreal, and it was all too real.

It was dreamlike, and it was nightmarish, and when she pinched herself and winced, she couldn't help but smile sadly.

This, she thought as she slipped into her coat and looked outside again, was how it had all started. Seeing shadows move under the trees down there.

Beginnings and endings, all blurred together in one vast wheel.

She sighed and left the room, walked down the hall, and knocked on Marty's door, opening it without waiting for an invitation.

"Hey," Marty said when Jennifer poked her head in, "you sure about this?"

"A sure winner," she assured the girl. Then she scanned the room and asked, "Where's Amy? I thought—"

"Cool it, Field, huh? We know what we're doing."

Jennifer hoped so. If they didn't, the only advantage she could think of would be irrevocably lost.

"Well?" Marty asked, her voice telling her either to say something or get out.

Jennifer cleared her throat. "Will it be done on time?"

Marty frowned at her in feigned rage. "Hey, what is this? Are you questioning the artist?"

"No, no, never."

"Then bug off, Field. I have work to do."

Jennifer saluted her and started to close the door.

"And, Field!"

"What?"

"If we lose, my homework for a month, right?"

"Right," she answered glumly and continued to hear the girl's delighted laughter as she went downstairs.

tomorrow

At the door she stood for a while watching others watch television. Pie was there; the girl didn't turn around.

Outside, she made a complete turn around the crescent before stopping in at the Union to call Conrad's house to see what was keeping him and Marysue. There was no answer even after a dozen rings, but she thought nothing of it. Whatever Conrad had wanted to pick up was evidently taking him longer than he had planned; unless, she thought as she stepped outside again, they were already on their way back.

Music from an open window; delighted laughter in front of one of the dorms.

Though she stayed away from the gaps between buildings, and couldn't help imagining movement just beyond the corner of her vision, she felt almost safe right then. Dramon's invitation had told her when and where he was going to make his next move, and she didn't think he'd do anything before then, not unless she was dumb enough to walk straight into his house again.

At least she hoped not.

He was mad, in both senses of the word, and everything depended upon his madness, and his anger, working with her instead of against her. He expected her to run; perhaps he thought she would strike back immediately. Patience was what she needed then.

Above her, in the star-flecked dark, a flock of Canada geese flew southward, their calls sounding of melancholy and distance. Another ending, she thought.

A second complete circuit around the crescent had her laughing at herself. If she were a cat, her tail would be twitching, and she'd be attacking every leaf blowing across her path.

She decided that it would be a good time, even the perfect time to go down to the gym to work off some of her excess energy. Otherwise, she'd be popping in on Marty all night, driving the girl crazy. Not even Zucco or

Marysue could calm her down, and sleep was going to be more important now than it had been for weeks.

She started down the path then, telling herself that courage had nothing to do with what she had planned. She was only being practical, only doing what had to be done. Being brave and foolhardy had nothing to do with it.

And even if they did, it was too late to stop now.

The noise to her right almost went unheard.

She looked down the slope, at the pools of white laid down by the lights along the path, and at the dark between them.

She stopped, and listened, and heard it again.

Something was moving out there, across the grass, just out of reach of the light.

The wind, she thought.

But there was no wind.

The night's chill deepened, and her breath fogged into a cloud in front of her face.

She moved on, and the noise followed her, stopping when she did.

Conrad, she told herself then; it's only Conrad, back and watching my flanks. Creeping around, trying to protect me.

The gymnasium complex looked very far away, the dim light over the door winking on and off as a branch of a young oak passed in front of it.

She took a step backward and stared into the dark, shading the side of her face with one hand to keep the light from ruining her night vision. A step had her off the path and onto the grass, and her eyes watered with the strain of her looking.

Nothing.

Not a sound.

Until she put her hand down and heard footsteps out there, not moving toward her, not moving away. Something pacing back and forth. Calmly waiting.

Back on the path again, she reversed her direction and started back up the slope.

Footsteps. Deliberately loud, but not so loud that she could dismiss them as a joke.

And then, just before she reached the first building, there was the breathing.

So soft she could barely hear it; so quiet she was tempted to blame the sound on the breeze that sprang up as she moved.

Soft, and quiet.

In. And out.

Sounding so close that she felt as if she could reach out and touch it, so close she felt as if she could feel its warmth across the back of her neck.

Him, she thought then. It's him. Watching me. Testing. Seeing if I'm going to run, or scream, or do something stupid like charge after him.

Into the dark.

Breathing in and out.

Footsteps scuffing over the grass.

Despite her conviction that he wouldn't do anything to hurt her until the next night, Jennifer's pulse began to quicken, and her own breathing grew shallow. But she wouldn't give him the satisfaction of running. Instead she continued taking normal strides, refusing to surrender to the urge to look around. He had seen her look once; she wouldn't look again.

And once she reached the top, she turned sharply onto the walkway and marched for her dorm, climbed the stairs calmly, and went straight to her room. She took off her coat and tossed it onto the bed. Left the lights off and walked over to the window.

He's out there, she thought looking down at the trees. Suddenly she wished Lee were there.

Twelve

SHE WOKE ON FRIDAY MORNING WITH THE FEEBLE hope that the previous few days had been nothing but a terrible dream, a reaction to all that had gone before. The hope died immediately, however, and she rolled out of bed, dressed, and realized suddenly that neither Marysue nor Conrad had tried to contact her the night before.

Beauford's door was locked when she tried it, and there was no response to her loud knocking.

She wasn't in the showers.

A nugget of dead cold settled in Jennifer's stomach. She questioned the other girls still stumbling sleepily around the hall, but no one had seen her since the day before.

Willing herself not to panic, she fetched her coat, went downstairs, and dialed the pay phone. It took her two tries to manage to dial Conrad's house; his mother answered on the first ring, somehow knowing who it was.

Five minutes later, numb and stiff, Jennifer replaced the receiver and walked outside, gasping at the cold wind that slapped across her face.

There had been an accident.

Not a serious one, Mrs. Chang had hastened to add, but an accident nevertheless. Apparently Marysue's car had lost its brakes as they were going down the hill into Staines. There was no estimate as to how fast the Thunderbird was going when it reached the bottom, but its size and speed made controlling the vehicle nearly impossible. It was, she was told, only Marysue's presence of mind that averted a tragedy: she managed to steer the car off the road and through a barbed wire fence that bordered one of the fields. It was, at the last, the rough ground that had slowed the car down.

Jennifer couldn't speak without choking.

Mrs. Chang told her the two were all right and in her house right then. Bruised and considerably sore from their banging around, but a day's rest would have them back to normal. She asked then if Jennifer would be able to come down and see them and also said she was sorry she hadn't contacted Jennifer about the accident, but she had been so distracted.

A car swept around the drive and backfired, causing Jennifer to jump.

Then she stared in the direction of the dean's house, and she felt him, actually felt him watching, felt him laughing at her, and the fear that was growing within her.

Testing, she thought. He's only testing you.

And as soon as she had taken a step toward the Student Union, she knew she was wrong.

It wasn't testing—he was making sure she had no allies.

He wanted her alone.

Despite the bright sunlight the day suddenly grew dark, the wind felt as if it were December.

She pushed her hands through her hair and bit down on her lower lip as she continued on, determined to put something in her stomach. She had to have strength. She had to be sure that wherever he was, he would see her going through the day as if nothing were wrong. Make your strength his weakness, she told herself as she ate. Make his madness your strength.

But time wasn't cooperating to hasten it all to completion.

The hours before noon moved in excruciating slow motion. Her classes seemed endless, and endlessly dull; the increasingly excited chatter about the evening's dance seemed shrill and mindless. And the only lift she had was when she called Lee.

"Much better," Andrew Fawkes told her. "He's not going to run the mile anytime soon, but he's feeling much better."

Jennifer grinned at the wall beside the telephone, and when Lee came on the line, the grin turned to a soft smile.

"You all right?" he asked.

"Yes."

"Are you—"

"Yes."

She heard him sigh, both in exasperation and reluctant admiration. "I heard about Zucco and Richmond."

She told him what she had learned from Mrs. Chang and waited until he had finished a long stretch of nonsense swearing before saying, "I'm going to miss you tonight."

"Then come down here instead," he answered quickly. "You can sign my bandage or something."

"I can't," she said. "You know that." A glance at the door, at the students passing by. Her voice lowered. "Even if I wanted to, I don't think he'd let me."

Lee swore again. "You're crazy."

"No," she said. "But he is."

Then she changed the subject, talking about anything and everything until his father called time. When the phone went dead, she stared at it for a while, then called the Changs, and was delighted when Marysue picked up the receiver.

"Oh," Marysue said, "it's you, is it?"

"Who else?" she said brightly.

"You should see my gorgeous face, Field. I look like an advertisement for bruise cream."

She laughed. "But are you okay?"

"How can you ask that? My baby tampered with and all scratched up, and Zucco moaning like a man who's broken every bone in his body—what a stupid question."

"What about tonight?" she asked.

"Forget it. Mrs. Chang is worse than a warden. I'm lucky she lets me out of bed to see what year it is."

Jennifer laughed and listened without comment to Marysue's complaints. Yet she was relieved that they had escaped serious injury and grateful to Mrs. Chang for insisting they get better before returning to campus.

It was almost twenty minutes before Beauford hung up. "The warden's back. Gotta get into my cell."

And when the receiver was replaced and Jennifer was outdoors again, she realized how terribly alone she was. In spite of the students rushing around, she felt as though she were a stranger there. And no one cared enough to ask if she needed assistance.

She went and ate lunch and tasted nothing.

She returned to the dorm, where Amy dragged her upstairs to show her the costume.

After that her expression hardened and the loneliness passed. And she walked back to the dining hall where, after fast-talking her way into the kitchen, she found what she wanted and slipped it into her pocket.

When she returned outside, she stood on the edge of the drive for a long time, staring at the dean's house. Not moving. Wanting him to see that she was still there.

Then, quite deliberately, she turned her back and walked slowly away.

It was time, she knew. It was time to begin.

The wind died with the sunset, leaving twigs scattered over the drive and leaves in shifting piles along the paths and walkways. Breath condensed on window panes. Voices carried fragilely in the night air.

And the harvest moon rose as a great tinted ball, setting loose the shadows that had been hiding in the hills.

The gymnasium had been wonderfully decorated: jack-o'-lanterns of every size and description lined the walls, skeletons and witches, black cats and ghosts dangled from the beams and swayed in the air currents that moved under the ceiling; orange and black streamers were everywhere, and the members of the rock band hired for the occasion were dressed in sequined costumes that caught the lights and threw them back as colored lances and shifting stars.

Along the wall by the main door were a pair of long tables set together and covered with an orange-and-black cloth. Bowls of punch, cans of soda, cakes, cookies—all in traditional shapes and colors.

But most amazing of all to Jennifer were the costumes themselves—from the thrown-together hobo with burnt cork face and tattered clothes, to the many elaborately detailed and obviously expensive ones that made the celebration less like a private school dance and more like a ball at Mardi Gras.

Queens and princes, demons and monsters, fairy tale characters and characters from popular movies moved among figures that were works of pure imagination: a butterfly with sparkling gossamer wings eight feet across, a caterpillar complete with varicolored segments and all its tiny, humorously shod feet, a hideously deformed creature whose face was covered with slime, a woman in a ball gown and a skeleton's head, a fly so unpleasantly perfect most people avoided it.

She was stunned by the sight. And she stood just inside the door, listening to the music blare from the loudspeakers, watching the dancing, hearing snippets of conversation as the revelers swirled around her. Several instructors were there as judges and chaperones. Most seemed more intent on devouring the snacks than in keeping order in the gym.

It was warm.

It was noisy.

And she had to remind herself more than once to stop wondering who was behind a mask. While the other students were there to have a good time and blow off steam after two months' grueling work, she was there to save her life.

She began a slow circuit of the huge room and was stopped more than once to explain to a classmate that she and the Visrans were there as a group. No one understood, and when she told them the joke, more than a few looked at her as if she were crazy.

She didn't care.

She was only glad that Marty and Amy had been amenable to the idea—the three little wolves in search of the big bad pig.

She glanced down at her arms and couldn't help but shiver. She had on a dark leotard, on the sleeves of which Marty had sewn fur that matched the mask that covered her head and neck completely. There was nothing more to the costume—except her jeans. But the effect, she hoped, would be the same as when Marty had accosted her in her room.

Moving constantly, then.

Watching the eyes, the way people walked, the way they stood.

He was there.

She knew it.

Somewhere in that mob, Peter Dramon was watching her and waiting to make his move.

The music grew louder, the dancing more frenzied.

Despite the fact that the doors were kept open to let in air, perspiration trickled down her spine and sides.

A Count Dracula and a bloated witch lurched past as she made her way to the front of the bandstand; she winced when she had to cross in front of the speakers. She joined a small laughing circle watching Tweedle-Dum and Tweedle-Dee do a comic turn in purple hula skirts, and as she watched she became resentful, angry that Dramon had taken even this pleasure from her.

She turned away sharply and stalked to the refreshment table, picked up a glass of punch and realized with a laugh that she'd have to take off her mask in order to drink. Then a pirate in a huge black cape handed her a straw and vanished into the crowd. A shrug and finally she fitted the straw past her muzzle to her mouth, and she drank with a silent sigh.

Where was he?

A second time around the room, jostled, waylaid, finally meeting Amy and Marty and standing against the wall while several people with small cameras took their picture. Marty was giggling, Amy muttered about the heat, but they had to admit that Jennifer's idea seemed to be working.

"Too bad we couldn't get a pig," Marty said.

Amy shrugged. "What can I say? Pie wouldn't do it."

And Jennifer laughed.

The music; the dancing; grotesque, beautiful, otherworldly faces swirling around her.

And suddenly, as if a switch had been thrown, it all became silent for Jennifer.

She saw him.

All around her eyes glittered, lips moved, and the band played drums, trumpets, and guitars without sounding a note.

He was there, in the middle of the floor.

For all that she was waiting for this moment, for all the rage she had been feeling and all that he had done to her friends, the sight of him stunned her. She leaned heavily against the wall and pressed a hand to her chest.

Watching her.

Fairies and giants and dwarfs and mythical beasts spinning by in slow motion.

She had wanted to unsettle him, but his gaze was steady.

The floor seemed to ripple, her legs buckled slightly at the knees.

She had wanted to throw a gauntlet in his face.
But he had tricked her.
Moving slowly toward her, gently pushing others aside.
He wore no costume.
He was a wolf.
Green eyes glowing.

Thirteen

THE DANCE AND ALL ITS NOISE RETURNED IN AN explosive rush, and Jennifer had to swallow hard to keep from screaming. Because her face was hidden, no one knew she was in distress, no one saw the horror flare in her doe-wide eyes as she watched him coming toward her.

And in that moment a flurry of images took her breath away—the first time she saw an alien without its human camouflage, an alien lab in the building in the woods, Dramon warning her off, an explosion, a gun, Lee bleeding, Marysue crying, and the faces of the dead the aliens left in their wake. And now her final suspicions were proven, her last fear realized.

The weight of the terror that had filled the past two months pressed her against the wall, and all her resolve, all her determination vanished the moment he at last stood before her, looking down and smiling.

The thing that used to be Peter Dramon.

"Good evening," he said, his voice husky and harsh. There was amusement in his eyes. "Your costume, Miss Field, is—interesting."

She couldn't speak, and beneath the mask she felt as if she were suffocating; she couldn't even bring herself to reach for the knife she'd stolen from the kitchen.

"Was it your intention to frighten me with that?" And he laughed, so quietly that none of the people near them heard it. "You are a fool," he said then. "What a magnificent fool you are."

She shifted to one side when he took another step closer, and he snapped out a hand to block her way.

"You're alone now," he whispered, leaning over, still staring. "You should have left when you had the chance."

A trembling began in her legs and in her hands that she had clasped in front of her. She tried to swallow and looked frantically around, trying to get someone's attention, to bring her over so she wouldn't be alone.

He laughed and shook his head. "It would be amusing, wouldn't it," he said, glancing over his shoulder, "if I won the contest. What a surprise they would get."

The band had gotten off the stage at the rear of the gym; a standing microphone had been set up. Behind it stood one of the physical education instructors, who was holding a clipboard in one hand, a large envelope in the other. She was attempting to make herself heard over the chatter and nervous laughter, attempting to explain the rules and describe the prizes for the costume contest.

"What a surprise," he repeated and instantly snapped out his other hand when Jennifer tried to slide out that way. "Don't," he warned sharply. "Not until I'm ready."

Suddenly she found her voice, though it was small and hoarse. "You tried to kill us."

He looked at her in astonishment.

His green eyes held hers for an endless moment. "You," he said. "The only one I'm going to kill now is you."

Her lips began to quiver, her eyes glistened with ready tears, and when he laughed yet again at her reaction to his presence, she found a crack in her terror and willed it to grow wider with the rage she'd once felt.

"The fire," she said. "You could have killed everyone at the Hilltop."

"As you killed us," Dramon returned. "I was hoping you'd see the parallel."

The phys. ed. instructor's explanations were finished, and she held up the envelope with the winners' names. Jennifer wanted to cry out then, to tell them what they had in their midst, but the alien seemed to read her mind—he turned until he was standing beside her and gripped her left arm. Painfully.

"When the music begins again," he said without looking at her, "we will have our own little dance."

Then, from out of the crowd standing around the dance floor, came the Visrans.

"C'mon, Jen," said Marty, grabbing her other arm. "We have to get up front."

Dramon didn't release her, and the twins seemed to notice him for the first time.

Amy looked him up and down scornfully. "Some people will do anything to keep from having an original idea, you know what I mean? Who did your costume? It looks so ratty!"

Dramon glared at her, but she'd already turned to Jennifer and repeated her sister's command. The word was, the three little wolves were among the finalists, and they had to be up front and ready when their names were called.

Jennifer nodded, yanked her arm free and started with them through the crowd. She stared straight ahead, feeling the alien's gaze on her back, realizing when she reached the stage that she had bought only a few minutes of time. Once the announcements had been made and the music restarted, he would come for her again.

But for then she was free, and it would give her time to think of some way she could use the weapon in her pocket.

The twins chattered nervously and applauded wildly as each category's runners-up and winners were announced, the lucky ones climbing onto the stage for all the others to see. Flashbulbs and electronic flashes burst from the sidelines. There were cheers, hoots, a few good-natured hisses and boos.

Jennifer heard nothing; she looked behind her and didn't see him. Suddenly the Visrans were shrieking, hugging each other and her, and dragging her hastily around to the three steps at the side of the stage. Third place, she thought she heard. Third place, and the twins were ecstatic.

The applause was thunderous, the cameras flashed lightning, but she focused on nothing but the figure of Peter Dramon, pushing away from the wall and making his way toward her. Grinning. Mockingly applauding. Angling toward the side where he could grab her when she came down.

No one stopped him.

The last winner was announced, and a tape was played over the speakers until the band could regroup.

No one stopped him.

Those on the stage congratulated each other, the twins jumping up and down in their excitement and, for the moment, forgetting Jennifer was there.

She couldn't move. Like a bird before a snake she could only watch him thread through the sudden blossoming of dancing, looking nowhere but at her. Still grinning. Now nodding.

Her left hand drifted to her pocket where it pressed against the hilt of the small, sharp knife. But she didn't dare take it out then; there were too many people around, and she had to be accurate the first time, or she wouldn't get another chance.

She tried moving to her left, but the drummer yelled at her to get off the stage, shaking his sticks at her and scowling as he called for the other band members to help her.

Dramon stood at the foot of the steps.

The dancing continued, the laughter, the noise.

Now, she thought; it has to be now

With her hand still pressed against her pocket she took a deep breath and suddenly yanked off her mask. Her hair fell to her shoulders, damp and stringy, she blinked against the bright lights, and someone shoved her in the small of the back.

The mask flew out of her hand as she stumbled forward, and by the time she regained her balance she was at the stage's edge, and Dramon was waiting there, a hand outstretched to assist her to the floor.

He was smiling.

A faint glow in his slanted green eyes.

Her heart pounded, her breath came in short gulps, and when he reached out and grabbed her left elbow, making it impossible for her to take out the knife, she took the steps quickly and kept on going, hoping to drag him off balance. But it didn't work because he turned nimbly and, pushing the butterfly to one side, forced her to march directly toward the main doors.

She didn't resist, and she knew that puzzled him. He looked down at her several times, waiting for a word, a sign, that she had something planned. But she kept her gaze straight ahead and a smile on her lips. Once outside, she thought, once outside it will be over.

Then, before she knew what was happening, the Count Dracula appeared on her right, veered in front of her and tripped, slamming into Dramon and making him loosen his grip. Jennifer just stood there for a second, gaping while the creature tried to apologize in mime for his clumsiness. Dramon only snarled and shoved him away, turned back to Jennifer, and suddenly gasped and bent over, arms folded across his stomach.

"Gee," the vampire said then, "I think he's in trouble."

Jennifer's mouth fell open, and her eyes widened when the bloated witch she had seen before whirled in the arms of the pirate and slammed into the alien, knocking him sideways through the crowd and up against the wall.

"Oops," said the witch, in a deep southern drawl. "Lord, I'm just so clumsy these days."

"But—but how?" Jennifer asked when the witch took off her mask and grinned, the vampire unmasked, and the pirate did as well.

"Later, Jen," Conrad said and pointed.

Dramon, seeing his four foes, staggered toward the door and abruptly broke into a shambling run that scattered dancers and watchers before him.

Jennifer, her mind burying all her questions, ran after him and, as soon as she reached the door, pulled out the knife.

She saw him running up the path, one arm still across his midsection, slowing him down. He was heading for the house, and she knew she couldn't let him reach it. Ordinarily he would have been much swifter than she, might not even have turned to run, but it was evident he had been thumped viciously in the side by Zucco, the side that held the patch that allowed him to breathe human air. And somewhere in that house she suspected was the means to revive him.

She ran, the glint of moonlight off the blade catching her eye, the sound of footsteps behind her tempting her to look around. But she refused to take her eyes off the creature ahead, angling now off the path and across the grass toward the dark that filled in the trees.

She followed.

It looked behind, saw her, and stumbled.

Redoubling her efforts, she fairly leaped off the path after it, stretching her legs, taking in the night air and ignoring the stabs of cold. She didn't know if she could do it once she reached the alien, didn't know if she could kill it, but her anger had taken over, and her hand gripped the knife tightly. She knew she wasn't carrying it just for show.

Suddenly it veered to the right as Conrad stepped out of the shadows, a baseball bat in one hand.

And veered back again when Marysue appeared, a bat in her hand as well.

They had flanked it, gone around it, and now it was trapped in a circle of moonlight beyond the lights of the school.

It snarled and straightened.

Jennifer slowed and stopped.

Green eyes glowing, and fangs bared and gleaming.

Conrad warned them all to be careful, and it spun on him and feinted a charge, but Conrad only lifted the bat higher. It moved toward Beauford, and she smiled without a shred of humor, holding her weapon up and daring it to try.

For a moment Jennifer was caught by the expressions on their faces, the hatred driving out fear, the resolve to end it there and then. Then she realized that it had turned to face her, and she felt someone at her back.

"Jenny."

A whisper. It was Lee, sounding weak.

She glanced at him just as his legs gave out and he crumpled to the ground, and without thinking she took a step toward him.

Marysue screamed.

She whirled, the knife out in front, as the alien howled and charged her, engulfed her in its arms and aimed its fangs at her throat. But its momentum knocked them backward and tripped them over Lee, and when they landed in a tangle of snapping jaws and thrashing legs, her arms were freed and she fought back, one elbow in its throat to hold its fangs at bay.

The noise seemed deafening.

The pains in her chest as if her heart were bursting.

And then, within the space of an eye blink, she was rolling free across the grass.

Swiftly she scrambled to her knees, the knife out in front, her other hand slapping the hair from her eyes.

The alien was struggling to stand, snarling, growling, holding its side.

Conrad and Marysue stood a few yards behind it, Lee on the ground between them, but they didn't move, they only watched as it finally swayed to its feet, its lower jaw sagging and its eyes growing dim.

Jennifer kept the knife out.

And the wolf-creature lowered its head, raised it again, and began to move toward her.

She didn't move.

It came on.

And as she pushed herself one-handed to her feet, it swerved to one side and vanished into the dark. Into the trees.

When Conrad started to chase after it, she held up a hand to stop him. It was dying. She had seen the blood flowing from its side, from the area of the patch where it had fallen against her knife; and she looked then at the stained blade, and with a grimace tossed it aside.

It was dying.

It was only a matter of time.

Fourteen

"YOU KNOW," LEE SAID, HIS GOOD EYE PARTIALLY closed, "if you didn't have those hairy arms, this could be a scene right out of *The Wizard of Oz.*"

The door to Conrad's mother's car was open and he was sitting on the edge of the passenger seat, one hand on the top of the door to steady him. Jennifer, Conrad, and Marysue were on the curb that ringed the parking lot.

"I suppose that makes me the brainless Tin Woodman," Conrad muttered.

"If the brain fits . . ."

"Well, child," Marysue said, fluffing her hair, "if I'm dear sweet Dorothy, what does that make poor Jenny?"

"Don't say it," Jennifer warned with a grin, and Lee, his blackened bandage serving as both pirate's eye patch and headband, lifted his hands in surrender.

Her grin softened then when he winked at her, and she draped her hands over her knees and looked up at the stars. She had no idea how much time had passed since the alien had stumbled away to die in the woods, but most of the lights in the dorms were long out, the visitors' cars gone, and the gymnasium dark and locked.

It was cold, but she barely felt it.

The moon was close to setting.

They had taken Lee straight to the dorm after the fight, and in the common room they made sure he was all right, that his injuries hadn't bled anew. He was, he insisted sourly, just fine, winded, that was all. But they had stayed there until the costumed party-goers had begun to drift back in. Then they had decided to go outside again.

To walk.

To think.

And they had finally ended up there at the car.

When Jennifer asked, Lee admitted that coming to the dance had been his idea. He had guessed Dramon would attend the dance, and he knew she would try to face Dramon on her own, and the longer he had lain in bed imagining it, the more he felt that he couldn't let her go alone. So after he'd talked his parents into taking in a movie, he called Zucco, and they arranged the rescue party.

"The trouble is," he said, "you sure didn't need it."

"Wrong," she said, getting up from the curb and walking over. "If you guys hadn't come, I—" The cold reached her then, and she didn't protest when he stood up and slipped an arm around her waist, hugging her tightly.

"My dear child," Marysue said, "hasn't it always been this way? I mean, I really mean, haven't I always had to get you out of the messes you've been in?"

Jennifer frowned.

"Well?" Marysue said.

"I'm thinking, I'm thinking," she told her and laughed when Beauford pretended to lunge at her.

Silence then, while Jennifer tried not to think about what would have happened if they had failed. What would Dramon have done if he'd killed her? Where could he have gone? How long could he have lived without full life-support systems?

Academic, she told herself then. It's all academic.

After so long, and finally, it was over. The last alien was gone. The last threat vanquished. Yet she didn't feel like a heroine; Dramon's body, she was positive, would never be found. He would vanish, someone else would take his place, and life at Thaler Academy would go on just as before.

As she would, working to get into college, spending time with Lee alone, and time with Lee and the others. Writing letters to her parents, doing papers, doing home-work, taking tests, and going to dances and parties.

She puffed out her cheeks and sighed, and looked at the others when she realized they were watching her.

"I know," Conrad said, a half smile parting his lips. "It's gonna seem awfully tame around here."

Marysue hugged his arm. "My dear boy, how can you say that when I'm around?"

"Like I said, tame."

And she smiled at him.

"Jen?" Lee said as he sat down again.

She crouched down, reached out, and ran a finger slowly along Lee's jaw. He was pale, and she knew that it was time for them to leave.

"You going to be okay?" he asked.

She nodded after a brief hesitation. "Yeah. I think so."

"My father still wants to make that dinner."

"You'll be lucky to see Christmas when he finds out you snuck out."

He grinned. "I'll get out of it."

"Oh, really?"

"Don't I always?"

And he kissed her. One that lasted a long time. And when she recovered and kissed him back, they didn't

separate until Marysue had slid behind the wheel, insisting that she drive. Conrad stood behind her, clearing
his throat.

"Call me tomorrow," Lee told her as the door was
closed and she stepped aside.

"Don't say that," Marysue ordered, turning the key,
starting the engine. "You know, Fawkes, that sometime
between now and then she'll get another one of her ideas,
and do you have any idea what kind of trouble we'll get
in then? We'll probably end up—"

"Drive!" Conrad said from the backseat.

And with a high, pealing laugh, she pulled away.

Jennifer watched and waved until the car was long out
of sight. She slipped her hands into her pockets and
started back for the dorm.

And stopped on the threshold.

What had that girl wanted to know that morning?
Something about acid rain in Germany?

She looked over her shoulder.

At the night, at the dark.

Then she shook her head sharply and went inside.

It's over, she reminded herself. It's all over, Field, and
you've got the whole weekend to recover.

She laughed then and clapped her hands as she ran up
the stairs. "Third place," she said delightedly. "Can you
believe it? I won third place!

www.ingramcontent.com/pod-product-compliance
Lightning Source LLC
Chambersburg PA
CBHW072006170626
46813CB00005B/2030